# SCOUTS' HONOR

## A NOVEL

## Carlos E. Cortés

AN INLANDIA INSTITUTE PUBLICATION

INLANDIA
INSTITUTE

RIVERSIDE, CALIFORNIA

*Scouts' Honor* by Carlos E. Cortés

Print ISBN: 978-1-955969-36-9
ePub ISBN: 978-1-955969-37-6
Library of Congress Control Number: 2025934639

Permissions
Inlandia Institute
4178 Chestnut Street
Riverside CA 92501

Printed and bound in the United States
Distributed by Ingram

Cover artist: Amaya Lawton
Author portrait: David Fouts
Book layout & design: Mark Givens
Publications Coordinator: Laura Villareal

Published by Inlandia Institute
Riverside, California
www.InlandiaInstitute.org
First Edition

# TABLE OF CONTENTS

## PART I
## LOLLY PATH

## PART II
## TROOP 64

# Part III
## Unfinished Story

# Part IV
## Parade Grounds

# Part V
## Golden Gate

# PART VI
# MOMENT OF TRUTH

# PART I

# LOLLY PATH

# CHAPTER 1

• • • • • • • •

# THE BODY

"Oh, shit," muttered Terry Fleener as he stumbled over something in the darkness on his way down the steep, rock-strewn path to the six-hole outhouse.

"Oh, shit!" he gasped when he realized he had tripped over a pair of legs.

"OH! SHIT!" he screamed when his flashlight caught the rigid face of fellow scout Harry Vincent.

# CHAPTER 2

# CAMP MATULIA

Dead bodies hadn't been all that common at Boy Scout Camp Matulia, so Harry Vincent quickly became the focus of scuttlebutt. Not that camp injuries didn't occur with relentless regularity. In fact, Camp Matulia, nestled in the rugged, forested, vigorously hilly southwestern corner of Missouri, was an accident waiting to happen. Consider the odds.

Four hundred and fifty young teenagers from big Kaioga City, one hundred miles to the north on the bend of the Missouri River, arriving every other Monday for a twelve-night camping session. Then dozens of adult volunteer leaders who accompanied their respective troops, mirrored by at least as many permanent camp staff. All traipsing around the chaotic hills covered with loose rocks and fallen branches, traversed by slippery, twisting dirt-and-pebbled paths on which scouts were supposed to walk, since camp safety rules prohibited running.

Of course mishaps occurred. Lots of cuts, bruises, splinters, and broken noses. Snake bites, like from copperheads who didn't appreciate being disturbed, and painful incursions by voracious ticks that eagerly attached themselves at night to delectable youthful scrota. Even an occasional finger chopped off by an errant axe while some kid was supposed to be learning to build a birdhouse for his Bird Study merit badge, required to earn promotion to Eagle Scout.

But Harry Vincent's dead body proved to be something special, really special. Since the Boy Scout Handbook didn't provide instructions about how to handle this kind of situation nor did the Scouts award merit badges for demonstrating skills in dealing with corpses, Harry's eerie presence on the lolly path created a new challenge for everybody, scouts and adult leaders alike. Improvisation, not customary rule-following, became the order of the day.

· · · · · · · ·

# CHAPTER 3

# MIKE MALDETH

Obviously there was an investigation later that hot, humid Thursday evening in 1948. Mike Maldeth, the Green River County Coroner, and young Deputy Sheriff Derek Pierson came out after they got Sheriff Lester "Pug" Jones' telephone call shortly before midnight.

"Mike, you'd better get right out to Matulia. They've got a dead body for you."

"A what?"

"Looks like one of those city kids fell down and managed to kill himself. Real scouts, they are. Those little dorks haven't got the faintest idea how to handle themselves in the woods. They ought to stay home with their mommies."

"Aren't you going out, too?"

"Hell, no. The Cardinals are still tied. They're in the bottom of the fourteenth inning. Great game. Pierson will meet you out there. Or he could swing by and pick you up."

"If it's not too much trouble."

"He'll be there in fifteen minutes." Pug paused. "By the way, Mike, make this one quick and clean. I've already heard from the folks in Kaioga City. They don't want anything sensational. Just a kid who died, OK. They'll handle the newspaper stuff." Pug paused again. "Of course, if you find something, you know, something unexpected, then we'll follow up on it. Not likely, though. You hearing me?"

"Hear you, Pug."

"I'll go there first thing tomorrow and check it out. Have fun."

*Sure, you asshole,* thought Maldeth. *You get to listen to the Cardinals. I get to scuffle around in the dark at Camp Matulia because of some lame-brained city kid.*

As he waited for the inexperienced Deputy Pierson, Maldeth marveled at the speed with which the Kaioga City bunch had swung into action. The camp leaders had probably called Andy Northcutt, the Kaioga City scout director, before they even notified the sheriff, most likely to get marching orders on how to handle the situation. *Well,* mused Maldeth, *let's see what we can find.*

When Coroner Maldeth and Deputy Pierson reached Camp Matulia, they had to make do with flashlights. Only a few of the rustic structures in the administrative complex had electricity. The rest of the camp muddled through in relative darkness.

They found the accident site illuminated by four Coleman lanterns, which bathed Vincent's body in a pale, off-white glow. The body had not been moved, so Vincent's legs still blocked the path down to the outhouse. Maldeth found himself laughing about the dozens of city boys pissing in their sleeping bags with no access to the latrine. Or maybe some of them had clambered down the dark hillside through the trees. Lucky if he didn't find another body before the night was over.

Maldeth took flash pictures of the body and then quickly inspected it. Yes, dead. At least the city folks got something right.

It didn't take long for Maldeth to reach a conclusion as to the cause of death. Harry Vincent had fallen and struck the back of his head on a rock, which had killed him, probably almost instantly. He must have stumbled on the slippery slope.

Most likely he wasn't concentrating on where he was walking, probably fantasizing about some nookie he never came near. The little virgin should have stuck to birds, snakes, and knot-tying.

There were some other cuts and bruises, most likely from the fall, including a nasty bump on his forehead. That's what happens when city boys without any experience start playing around in the woods. He'd call Pug Jones tonight when he got home—hopefully wake up the lazy son of a bitch—and write up the report first thing in the morning. Just like Pug ordered, just like the Kaioga City folks wanted, quick and clean.

\* \* \*

It was nearly nearly 2 a.m. when Maldeth informed the adult leaders of his conclusion, but few of the Troop 64 scouts had fallen asleep. Most had been watching the ghostly proceedings from the darkness of their tents clustered on the hillside. And, despite adult injunctions not to leave their tents, boys had been slipping back and forth among the tents spreading speculation about what was going on. In the process they contributed to a growing corpus of snotty adolescent interpretations about what had taken place earlier that evening.

Accidental death, huh? A freak incident, huh? Well, freak accidents do happen, but not usually on the path going down to the infamous six-hole outhouse referred to as "Lola's Lolly," a title whose origins nobody seemed to know. Maybe she was the first local girl some scout had banged in that shed in a year now faded into antiquity. But who in the hell would want to bang anyone in that stinking place, where veteran scouts would take first-year greenhorns to put them through their Camp Matulia initiation rites?

As the evening wore on, the jokes turned surlier, particularly after they learned about the coroner's ruling—that Harry had died from hitting his head on a rock. That Green River guy obviously didn't know his ass from a hole in the ground. He should have at least considered the possibility that Harry might have died from an overdose of breathing while he was in Lola's Lolly. That hick certainly never set foot in the outhouse or inhaled its fumes. Or maybe people from Southwest Missouri were just so used to the smell of shit that he never even gave it a thought.

By the time the sun came up, the shock of Harry's death was cavorting madly with the ugliness of adolescent toilet humor. Yet only one scout, someone in the Snake Patrol, dared utter what must have been on lots of their minds: "It's about time that little prick Vincent got his."

# CHAPTER 4

# HAWK TENT

The Hawk Patrol tent was not a particularly pleasant place to be that Thursday night nor the next day. Harry Vincent had been one of their bunkmates. Now his sleeping bag and duffle bag dominated the tent, ominous reminders of what had transpired. When would the leaders get that stuff out of there? Not until Saturday, they learned, when Harry's folks would be down to pick it up.

Like most of the Matulia shelters, the Hawk tent consisted of a raised wooden platform covered by two canvas roofs that sloped down in opposite directions from a long beam running the length of the tent and supported by front and back vertical wooden pillars. The two canvas roofs ended about three feet above the floor, at which point vertical flaps dropped straight down to the edges of the platform. These side flaps remained fastidiously rolled up at all times except when it rained, when they would be untied and lowered to provide protection.

Harry's bunk, the standard Matulia iron cot, sat second from the right of the four beds that stood parallel to each other in the rear of the tent, all heads against the back flaps. Those beds belonged to the four fourteen-year-olds who had joined Troop 64 and become Hawks two years earlier in the spring of 1946, when they all turned twelve and became eligible to move up from the Cub Scouts. Pensive Greg Brooks slept in the far right position, then Harry, then gangly patrol leader Chucky Karlson, and finally big Duster Fertig on the left. At the front of the tent sat the bunks of the two newcomers, thirteen-year-old Freddy Collins and twelve-year-old Benny Green, only two months removed from the Cubs.

As per instructions, each scout brought a sleeping bag to place on his cot and a duffle bag filled with clothes and miscellaneous items, like toiletries and scout knives. Since scouts lived out of those duffle bags for two weeks, neatness was at a premium, guaranteed by the adult leaders' multiple daily tent inspections.

Predictably, the five remaining Hawks got little sleep that night. The following morning, Freddy and Benny, the two younger boys, took off early for breakfast in the camp mess hall, leaving the three older Hawks to square away Harry's belongings.

Looking down at Harry's unused sleeping bag, Chucky voiced what he figured they all had been thinking. "It sure won't be the same without Athos." Greg and Duster merely grunted. All three avoided eye contact.

# PART II

# TROOP 64

· · · · · · · ·

# CHAPTER 5

# VOICE FROM THE PAST

It had been an unrewarding afternoon for Charles Karlson, M.D. More patients than he liked to treat, but that boring Irene Blatchett had insisted on seeing him for her emergency, which, of course, it wasn't. And he didn't realize how long it would take to drain the wax out of Daniel Murphy's ear. What a way to spend an afternoon after a long morning of surgery!

It was getting dark when Karlson sat down to peruse his business mail. The Golden Gate Bridge seemed unusually dramatic at dusk. He loved the awkward angle of the setting sun, which sliced through the San Francisco mist, making it difficult for him to stop watching the interplay of colors.

Karlson tossed envelope after envelope into the waste basket: charity requests for fighting every imaginable as well as newly invented disease; offers of special rates for medical magazines he didn't know existed, much less cared about; announcements of purported, expensive wonder drugs. Not in the mood. Fortunately Missy handled his personal mail at home, so when he got there he could just settle down with a good book, although he really hadn't done that in quite some time. Oh, well, a Giants' game would do for intellectual stimulation.

Karlson was about to toss the unopened *Chicago Telegram* subscription letter when he noticed what appeared to be a personally typed name above the institutional return address: A. Cunningham. Intrigued, Karlson carefully clipped the edge of

the envelope in his always precise manner and gently extracted the letter. It got to the point very quickly.

*Dear Dr. Karlson:*

*You may not remember me, since we've actually talked only
once. It's been thirty-six years since you and I spoke at Boy
Scout Camp Matulia in the summer of 1948. Actually we
did meet briefly a second time at an Eagle Scout ceremony in
Kaioga City later that same year. You received your Eagle
that day.*

*My name is Ardith Cunningham. It used to be Ardith
Millett when I was a reporter at the Kaioga City Tribune. I
came down to Camp Matulia to interview you and some of
the others who had known Harry Vincent before he died that
summer.*

*Let me get right to the point. I am now a columnist at the
Chicago Telegram, and I am writing a book called
"Unfinished Stories" about the most intriguing stories I've
ever covered. This might seem strange to you, but one of those
stories was the one I wrote about the Harry Vincent case.*

*I'm interviewing as many Troop 64 leaders and Hawk
Patrol members as I can. I've also been in contact with Ruth
Vincent, Harry's mother, who is helping me with the story.*

*I will be coming out to San Francisco for a conference this
spring and would like to speak with you about the Vincent incident, particularly what you recall about the day he died. I
understand from his mother that you two were very good
friends.*

*Please let me know if I can meet with you. I'll call in a few
days to see about setting up an appointment. I hope this works
for you.*

*Sincerely,*
*Ardith Cunningham*

Karlson stared at the letter, then at the Golden Gate Bridge,
then at the letter again, then back out the window. Of course
he didn't want to talk about Harry Vincent again. He certainly

didn't want to talk to this Ardith Cunningham, who used to be Millett. Karlson tried to conjure up an image of the reporter, that Millett girl, but all he could recall were her uninspiring nondescript face and her even less inspiring, even more nondescript boobs. He did remember her asking lots of questions and his giving short, vague answers, while keeping a close watch on the other Hawks to make sure they didn't say too much. He had taken pride in that moment of true Boy Scout leadership.

But that happened thirty-six years ago. Why in hell did this damn woman want to discuss something from way back when he was a kid? He had built a wonderful life in San Francisco. Why did she have to start digging up the past and maybe screw things up? Why couldn't she just get on with her own fucking life?

Karlson returned to the letter. Her words struck him: "the Harry Vincent case"; "the Vincent incident." Why did she call it a "case"? Or an "incident"? What did she know now that she didn't back then?

Karlson tried to picture Ardith whatever-her-name-was. Ardith Millett. That scrawny, pale-skinned girl with a timid voice who kept asking the same questions over and over. *How well did you know Harry? What is your favorite Harry story? When was the last time you saw him? Where were you when he died?*

Back then he hadn't told her much. Neither had the other Hawks. They had promised the adult leaders—under Scout's Honor—that they would keep their answers short, that they wouldn't tell stories about Harry. But what about now? After so many years, some of them might blab. And if they did, then he, Charles Karlson, might come out looking like a liar if he refused to say anything or, worse yet, said something that conflicted with what she learned from the others. Karlson could see the pages of her new book.

While most of the other Hawks were glad to share stories about Harry Vincent, Dr. Charles Karlson, now a noted San Francisco orthopedic surgeon, who treats the Bay Area's rich and famous, refused to talk. What is he trying to hide? Why is he hiding it? What more does he know about Harry's death? Maybe he saw Harry Vincent die. Maybe he was there when it happened. Maybe…

No, thought Karlson, she would never write anything like that. *At least I don't think she would.* Not that skinny girl with no boobs.

Maybe he ought to just refuse to speak with her. Bad idea. She's going to write *something*. He'd look worse if he turned her down. As much as he hated the idea, he had to meet with her. He had to tell his side of the story, but not all of the story. How much of the story? Well, he had time to get ready. He damn well better get ready.

Karlson stared at the wall with his various degrees and honors, all neatly if somewhat ostentatiously framed. Then he reached down, unlocked the lower right-hand drawer of his desk, reached inside, and withdrew a small frayed blue linen case. Snapping it open, Karlson looked at his Eagle Scout pin. He hadn't taken it out in years. Slowly stroking it, Karlson remembered how proud he had been when he received it. Proud, but reserved.

Karlson took out an envelope of old, faded black-and-white photographs. Flipping through them he came to the one he wanted, a photo of four boys in scout uniforms, two grinning, one serious, almost solemn, and one, Harry Vincent, looking innocent while holding up his hand so that his raised middle finger protruded from the top of Greg Brooks' head.

The Musketeers, Karlson mused. The "Four Musketeers." How swell the other three had been, taking him in after he moved into their clannish, insular neighborhood, an awkward kid from tiny Merona, a farming town in western Kansas. How much he had loved being a Musketeer. Until the summer of 1948.

Karlson returned the badge and photos to the drawer and carefully locked it. Clicking on his tape recorder, he dictated a letter to Ardith Cunningham. When he finished, he felt an un-expected sense of relief. After thirty-six years of silence, he really did want to tell his story. At least part of it.

CHAPTER 6

• • • • • • • •

# THE FOUR MUSKETEERS

For years, Chucky Karlson, Duster Fertig, Gregory Brooks, and Harry Vincent had been known by everybody as the "Four Musketeers." Well, not really. In fact, they were the only ones who called themselves by that name.

Actually, Harry, Duster, and Gregory had chosen the "Three Musketeers" name when they entered kindergarten at Jonathan Norwood Elementary School. Already tight friends from growing up together in a two-block stretch of Randolph Road, they seriously considered and then finally approved the addition of shy, awkward Chucky Karlson, whose family had moved into their tight neighborhood at the beginning of third grade. After all, the original Musketeers—Athos, Porthos, and Aramis—had grudgingly accepted the hayseed D'Artagnan when he came to Paris. Chucky, complete with his western Kansas drawl, could join as "D'Artagnan," the outsider.

The four kids regularly hung out together. They'd do all kinds of things, like go to high school basketball games at the Municipal Auditorium or smoke in Harry's garage where they hid their cigarettes in the rafters or swim nude in the Little Blue River if they could hitch a ride with some of the older guys or sit around together playing with themselves while they fantasized about girls, especially older girls with big jugs, or go from house to house singing discordant Christmas carols and then stand there waiting to get paid for their imposed serenade.

But as they grew older the best times were Saturday nights when they would often camp out, sometimes in the hills above Sweeney Park, sometimes in a farmer's field, usually with his permission. They would laugh, smoke, tell jokes, and lie to each other about girls, like how one of them had copped a quick feel on the playground from Meredith Saunders, who had the biggest boobs in the seventh grade except for Blimpy Backster, the fattest guy in school.

The Vow was born during one of those Sweeney Park camp-outs, after they had played touch football in the afternoon (two hands below the waist, but no nut grabbing), finished their dinners of half-cooked burgers and lukewarm beans, and got tired of shining their flashlights in the windows of parked cars to see if they could catch anyone in the act. As they sat around the campfire they had built between their pair of two-man tents, they came up with the idea of the Musketeers' Vow. Actually, Greg Brooks came up with the idea, as he often did, which is why they dubbed him "Aramis," the low-key, cerebral Musketeer.

"Look," he said, after the boys had shared a rare period of long silence, "we're not just friends. We're the Musketeers. One for all and all for one. We need a vow, a Musketeers' Vow."

Fortunately, Chucky Karlson had come ready for action, meaning a pencil and paper. His folks had taught him that, as an outsider, he had to make an extra effort to belong. Be pre-pared, the Scout Motto said. In this case he was. Chucky couldn't remember why he had packed a pencil and a small pad in his knapsack. Maybe to leave "please rescue us" notes in case they got lost, which was unlikely since they were only a few minutes from civilization.

They worked late into the night, drawing up a list of things they should swear to and then argued over which ones to keep and which ones to eliminate. Each promise began with "I swear I," followed by the action they would or would not take.

At first they wrote down every suggestion. Some were serious, like "I swear I will never lie to a fellow Musketeer." Others not so serious, like "I swear I will never grab a fellow Musketeer's balls" or "I swear I will never fart in another Musketeer's slecping bag," which they quickly scratched. What's the use of camping out if you couldn't have fun.

Duster Fertig added the most important provision: "I swear I will never rat on a fellow Musketeer." The others always paid attention when Duster spoke. He was the most ominous of the four and by far the biggest. In fact, he was scary big, which is why he became "Porthos," the giant Musketeer.

"Never?"

"Never!"

"Even to our parents?"

"Never!"

"Even to my minister?"

"Never!"

"Even when I pledge Scout's Honor?"

"Never!"

"No matter what we do?"

"Never! You never rat on a fellow Musketeer."

By then it had turned into a game, taking turns topping each other with increasingly bizarre non-ratting scenarios, then all loudly chanting "Never!" in unison. Their imaginations ran wild.

"Even if one of us robs a bank?"

"Never!"

"Even if one of us shoots a policeman?"

"Never!"

"Even if someone takes a crap on the church floor?"

"Even if you screw someone's sister?"

"Especially if you screw *Greg's* sister. You get a bravery merit badge for that one."

You could always count on Harry Vincent to go too far and come up with something gross. That's one of the reasons why Harry was so popular with the other Musketeers and also one of the reasons he could piss people off, even fellow Musketeers. He wasn't exactly an imposing leader like Athos, his namesake, but he had plenty of style and imagination, particularly when it came to getting himself and the Musketeers into trouble. Although funny and outrageous, Harry usually didn't know when to stop. Or maybe he just didn't care.

The jokes ended after Harry insulted Greg's sister. You could tell when someone had gone too far with serious Greg because he would look down at the ground and say nothing or, when he was really angry, he would glare at the offender, turn his back, and walk away. This time he just gave Harry the middle finger, a serious middle finger. Before things could get out of hand, Chucky brought their focus back to The Vow.

"OK, 'One for all and all for one' means I will never rat on a fellow Musketeer. OK?"

"Make that Number One on the list," demanded Duster. "It's the most important promise."

When the others nodded, Chucky circled the statement and drew an arrow to the top of the page. The boys sat staring into the embers, maybe contemplating the possible implications of that guaranty.

"Are we up to it?" asked Chucky.

They all nodded. For a change, Harry didn't make a snide remark. In fact, he was the one who came up with the idea of swearing allegiance to The Vow by touching a hot ember with the tips of their right index fingers. After they'd all done it and screamed "shit" enough times and poured water on their fingers and sucked on them because they hurt like hell, they sat somberly until Harry broke the silence.

"I don't think even Greg's sister would dig a finger like this one."

Nobody laughed. Greg focused on the ground. Big Duster looked at Harry without smiling. Harry felt relieved that he was sharing a tent with Chucky.

# CHAPTER 7

# MUSKETEER SIGN

Not long after their camp-out, the four boys decided they needed a secret Sign to go with The Vow.

They had gathered, as usual, at Martin Andrews' house for their weekly patrol meeting. Actually, Martin was better known as "Cuddles" because of his dour, humorless personality. At sixteen, two years older than the Musketeers, he reigned as Hawk Patrol leader.

Patrol meetings generally followed a pattern, moving from discussions about what merit badges they could earn together and where they would hold their next camp-out to more important stuff like what girls they had goosed that week in the hallway. But this time Cuddles seemed even more serious and uncomfortable than usual. Finally, without a whit of foreplay, he broke the news.

"Look, you guys, we're getting a new member next week."

"A new member?" shouted Harry. "That'll screw things up."

"We don't have any choice. Tux Harrison said we needed more members and assigned one. And we're probably going to get more since I'm moving up to the Lordly Lions this spring."

"What a dorky patrol leader you turned out to be, Andrews. Couldn't you have just told old Tux to shove it?"

The Musketeers looked at each other with a sense of violation. What would they do now that their secret society had been pierced? It was OK that Cuddles Andrews wasn't a

Musketeer, but how were they going to deal with a new outsider? And what would Tux Harrison, the Troop 64 scoutmaster, do next?

"Do we know him?"

"No, his name is Freddy Collins. He just joined the troop. He'll be here next week. He's a seventh grader at St. Matthew's."

"St. Matthew's? You let Tux Harrison stick us with a Catholic?"

"You suck, Andrews. I can't wait for them to make you a Lordly Lion."

Actually, all of the boys hoped to become Lordly Lions someday. As the troop leadership patrol, the Lions got to do all of the good stuff, like be in charge of troop camp-outs and choose what the troop was going to do at the annual Kaioga City Boy Scout Roundup at the Municipal Auditorium. But they also knew they had to wait their turn.

When the four Musketeers gathered in the Hobo Forest that Saturday afternoon, it was all seriousness as they plotted how they were going to welcome Freddy Collins.

"What do we do now?"

"We've got to get prepared."

"How?"

"Old Tux sure screwed the Hawk Patrol."

"What do we do with the new kid?"

"He sure as hell can't become a Musketeer."

The four of them considered that dilemma. Responsibility wasn't something any of them wanted. They'd rather have fun. Why be a Musketeer if you have to be responsible?

"We need a secret sign," said cerebral Greg.

"A what?"

"A secret sign."

"Why?"

Greg paused as he pondered the details.

"If we have a sign, then we can signal each other to close ranks against the enemy."

"Yeah, that's good. Like the Musketeers did when Cardinal Richelieu's men would attack them and they'd fight back to back."

"But who's our enemy?"

"Cuddles Andrews?"

"Tux Harrison?"

"The new kid?"

The boys contemplated the challenge. What's the use of a secret sign if you didn't have an enemy.

"Everyone who isn't a Musketeer."

Duster's words provided a new sense of seriousness to the afternoon. They realized they were on the verge of a major life transition.

"Everyone? That's a lot of people."

"We can't fight everyone."

"We don't have to fight everyone," Chucky injected. "The sign would just be a secret way to tell each other that there's real danger out there."

"And we need to remember the Musketeers' Vow!" Duster jumped in.

Greg looked at his extended index finger, the one he and the others had pushed into the coals to swear their allegiance to The Vow. Then, slowly, he closed the thumb and index finger until the flat parts of their tops came together, as if picking up cake crumbs. He held them together, tightly, then looked up at the others for approval.

Duster smiled and nodded his head. "That's it." He pressed his huge thumb and index finger together. Chucky and Harry followed his lead until all four boys were making the sign.

"Just put your thumb and finger together, as if you're holding something really small."

"Yeah, like Karlson's pecker."

The others ignored Harry's remark. Chucky took the lead from Greg. "So anytime there's danger, all we have to do is press our fingers together to let the others know they need to be aware and remember the Musketeers' Vow. Watch out for each other. Protect each other. Never rat on each other."

Chucky looked around before continuing. "So if we're having a meeting and Cuddles Andrews tries to get us to do something stupid or that new kid—Collins—comes up with some shitty idea, all you have to do is press your thumb and finger together and we know what to do."

"Do we need to lift our hands when we make the sign?"

"No, we can keep them at our side so nobody else see's it."

"That means everybody has to be aware, all the time."

"Well, that's what you do when you're a Musketeer."

Duster made the sign and held it out in front of him. "OK, everybody touch up and swear."

The other three followed his lead, closing thumbs and index fingers, then thrusting their hands forward until the four signs came together.

"I swear," said Chucky. The others followed suit. Even Harry remained serious, helped by the fact that the others glanced at him with "keep your wise-ass mouth shut" looks. But the silent question remained: What was going to happen the first time one of them invoked the Musketeer Sign in a tough situation? Would they be able to hold things together? There was no way the boys could have envisioned what lay ahead of them that summer at Camp Matulia.

# CHAPTER 8

# OUTSIDERS

The Four Musketeers weren't particularly thrilled by the Scoutmaster Tux Harrison's decision to assign two new boys to the Hawk Patrol. Sure, they knew it was coming, ever since Arnie Hendrix had to quit the patrol just because his family was moving across the state to St. Louis. Now Cuddles Andrews had been promoted to the Lordly Lions leadership patrol, leaving only four Hawks. But they had been hoping Tux would choose people they liked.

Instead Tux had stuck them with a Catholic, Freddy Collins. And the Musketeers became even more irate when they learned that Tux had screwed them again by assigning them Benny Green, one of the few Jews in Troop 64. Why in hell didn't he join the synagogue troop? They didn't need this kind of crap.

Chucky Karlson, who had replaced Andrews as Hawk Patrol leader, probably because he was the oldest member, called a meeting of the Musketeers. He haltingly explained that they couldn't do anything about Harrison's action. They were going to have to take Green, too.

"That's not even his real name," snorted Harry Vincent. "When he started second grade at Norwood, he was Benjamin Greenberg. Little Benny Greenberg. Little dorky Benny Greenberg. Who in the hell does his family think they're fooling with this Green nonsense?"

"Yeah," big Duster Fertig jumped in. "Why do they all want

to hide who they really are? Are they afraid of something? Where do they think they are, Nazi fucking Germany?"

"Does that mean we're going to have to change all the food we eat at meetings?" Greg Brooks pondered. "What a drag! Why do they have to screw things up for everyone?"

"Look, guys," said Chucky. "It's not all that bad. Benny's a pretty nice kid. I think he'll fit in if we give him a chance."

"Greenberg fit in?" sneered Harry. "Why does he have to fit in? Can't he just go somewhere else? Listen, Merona Boy, can't you just tell old Tux that this isn't the place for Greenberg? That's what *you're* supposed to do. That's the kind of stuff we thought you'd do when we let you become patrol leader. D'Artagnan wouldn't have put up with this shit!"

"Yeah, Chucky," added Greg. "First Cuddles lets Tux Harrison shove Freddy Collins down our throats, like we needed a Catholic. Now you let him force us to take a Jew. Next thing you know he'll try to stick us with Mex Martinez. It's a good thing the Scouts make Negroes have their own troops or you'd be begging Tex to give us one of them. I guess that's what happens when you let a hick be your patrol leader."

There was a long silence as the Musketeers contemplated the decline of the Hawk Patrol. As too often happened, without warning, Chucky suddenly felt like an outsider. Harry broke the silence.

"At least Greenberg's probably circumcised."

The other boys howled at Harry's astute observation. One good thing about Jews is that they cut off their foreskins like normal people. Not Catholics, who all walked around with that ugly meat hanging down like cavemen.

"Have you ever seen Collins' pecker?"

"Who in the hell would want to look at it?"

"Or touch it."

"Except Duster," observed Harry. "He's been dying to hold

it. Probably wants to whack him off to see what happens when you hold all that meat."

"Shut your damn mouth, Vincent."

"OK, Duster. Don't get upset. Can't you take a joke?"

"I'm getting tired of your jokes."

The boys grew silent, as they considered the fate of the Hawks. First a Catholic, then a Jew. What next?

"The real Musketeers would have never put up with this."

"Weren't they Catholic?" serious Greg contemplated.

That observation seemed to perplex them. At least they thought for a few seconds before Harry wised off again.

"Yeah, but they stuck it to Cardinal Richelieu."

"Right, they probably weren't real Catholics, like Richelieu's men."

"Maybe the Musketeers were really Jews."

"Yeah, one of them was actually named Greenberg. Probably Aramis. He always seemed kind of sly."

"Aramis was not Jewish!" shouted Greg, his alter ego. "He was French, pure French. Nothing Jewish about him."

"Maybe Greg's really Jewish, too."

"Lay off, Harry!"

"Maybe his name's not really Brooks. Maybe it's Bernstein."

"Yeah, Gregory Bernstein. His father's actually a rabbi."

"They probably speak…what's that language?"

"You mean Hebrew?"

"Right, Greg probably speaks Hebrew at home."

"To hell with you guys. I'm going."

"Take it easy, Greg," Chucky jumped in. "They're just having fun."

"I've about had enough fun for one day."

"OK, let's get down to business," Chucky said seriously.

"Look, we've got Freddy Collins. Now we're going to have to take Benny Green."

"Greenberg!"

"We've got to make them feel at home."

"Listen, D'Artagnan. It's up to you to tell Tux that this is it. Enough is enough. No Mex Martinez. No Italians. And damn well no Negroes. We're the Boy Scouts of *America*, not the United fucking Nations. The Hawks need to stand for something."

Chucky saw this as his opportunity.

"Look, you guys. If you promise to try to make Freddy and Benny feel at home, I'll talk to Tux Harrison and tell him that this is enough. OK?"

The other three reluctantly nodded, but Harry had to add, "I'll be nice to Greenberg. But when we're at Matulia, I'm not going to sleep next to "Foreskin" Freddy Collins. Let Greg do that. He's dying to sleep next to his caveman pecker."

Greg gave Harry a dirty look but didn't have the energy to say anything more. That was Harry.

"You swear as Musketeers?" Chucky said, pressing his thumb and forefinger together.

Reluctantly, one by one, they made the Musketeer Sign. Then, after an appropriate silence, Harry added, "But the two of them still have to go through greenhorn initiation this summer."

Chucky nodded in agreement. Nobody escaped rookie initiation during their first year at Camp Matulia.

CHAPTER 9

• • • • • • • •

# SHORT SHEETING

Because the Musketeers had other priorities, the two green-horns escaped hazing during the first day at Camp Matulia that June of 1948. Troop 64's three adult leaders became the immediate Hawk targets.

The opening escapade began late that Monday afternoon after the troop had moved into its Matulia compound, an irregularly spaced collection of nine tents perched on a steep, forested incline. A huge grassy mesa, known as the "Parade Grounds," sat to the east of the compound. To the west lay a jungle of rocks and trees, sloping sharply down the hill to Lola's Lolly; a slippery zigzag trail provided access for boys courageous enough to avail themselves of this legendary house of unimaginable odors.

Eleven other tent compounds surrounded the Parade Grounds on three sides. For the next two weeks they would house the other troops that had come down from Kaioga City for this session. To the south of the compounds rose the rustic administrative center featuring the squat director's cabin, the knotty health lodge, and the cavernous mess hall, as well as the camp swimming pool. Beyond the administrative center lay a long, winding trail that led out to the general council ring, a rough wooden amphitheater of tiered benches, where the entire camp would gather several times a session for evenings of songs, Indian dancing, and tales of Matulia lore. Further on sat The Overlook, a high, flat, rocky bluff that dropped straight down six hundred feet to the Green River, which gave the county its name.

When the bugle sounded announcing time for everyone to converge on the mess hall for the session's first meal, the Musketeers swung into action. As usual, Harry Vincent organized the foray. He needed help, but the other Musketeers were happy to oblige.

The Hawks targeted the three Troop 64 adult volunteer leaders who had come down to supervise the troop for the two-week session. The three shared the leaders' tent, nestled against the Parade Grounds slightly distant from the troop's other tents and as far as humanly possible from Lola's Lolly. On good days this also meant upwind.

The leaders' tent was only marginally larger than those occupied by the individual patrols, but because it housed only three adult leaders, they enjoyed a bit more gracious space. They also benefited from the luxury of solid wooden beds with sheets, blankets, and mattresses.

Harry presented his plan. They would wait until the rest of the troop headed for the mess hall, then quickly ascend to the leaders' tent and short-sheet one of their beds.

Harry had become a master at short sheeting. This quick but deadly process consisted of pulling back the covers of someone's bed and then sewing the top and bottom sheets together horizontally about a quarter of the way up from the foot of the bed. In the best of all possible worlds, the victim would climb into bed, forcefully extend his legs, and unexpectedly jam them into the attached sheets with his knees still about half bent. The results could range from ripped sheets to a stubbed toe or sprained ankle, depending upon the force of his legs and the firmness of the attachment.

Harry had honed the skill of sewing quickly and firmly, if not particularly aesthetically. With the adults heading to the mess hall along with the rest of the troop and the other Musketeers standing watch, Harry slipped into the leaders' tent and rapidly worked his magic on one of the beds. It didn't make much difference whose bed it was. Fortunately, from their perspective, it belonged to long Bill Perryman, a tall and officious thirty-something whom they considered to be such a prick that they had named him "Putz" Perryman. Because Putz happened to feel the same way about Harry, their relationship had grown into a virtual blood feud.

The fact that the four boys arrived a few minutes late for dinner led to only a minor admonishment. The "we-had-to-go-to-the-lolly" excuse seemed to work just fine, at least for the time being. Moreover, boisterous camp director Alfred "Rocky" Reynolds always droned on that first night with welcoming remarks, introductions of the camp staff, and his blaring personal rendition of the nauseating official camp song, "Matulia, You'll Always Remain in My Heart." This helped make the Musketeers seem merely part of the stragglers from various troops. Nevertheless, they received a brief tongue-lashing from Putz Perryman, while managing to stifle their smirks.

It was still light—dusky light—when dinner ended and everyone headed from the mess hall to the main camp council ring, which lay in the opposite direction from the troop compounds. The council ring consisted of a multi-tiered set of wooden benches that encircled a big central area except for one small opening through which scouts entered and departed. Several times in every session the council ring played host to gatherings of the entire camp, with a massive campfire built in the center to light the proceedings. With luck—meaning not too many scouts with big butts—there was room for everyone.

Camp Director Rocky Reynolds always put on a good show that first night, with Indian dancing by camp veterans, stories of camp lore, and group singing. Sincere enthusiasm overflowed as the troops headed back to their compounds. Relaxing in their tent, the Musketeers eagerly awaited the moment that leaders bellowed "lights out." They then talked quietly, keeping an eye on the leaders' tent. When the leaders finally doused their Coleman lanterns, the boys waited and hoped. Fate delivered, big time.

"Shit!" came a scream from the leaders' tent, informing the Musketeers that they had struck pay dirt. Really struck, because the scream came from Bill Perryman. He was the only adult leader who regularly employed such language, at least at camp, even though he usually tried to restrain himself and maintain the leaders' expected decorum around the boys. The short sheet had brought out the true Putz Perryman.

That was the one and only "shit," but it was more than enough to make their escapade worth the effort. On went the Coleman lanterns in the leaders' tent. It hadn't yet started raining, so the side tent flaps were still up. From their tent the boys could see the leaders gathered around Perryman's bed, inspecting the damage. So could the other tents.

Perryman ripped his bed apart and inspected Harry's handiwork. He must have uncoiled his legs with considerable force, because his eyes darted from his stubbed toe to his shredded sheets. Harry had hit a daily double.

"Somebody must have short-sheeted Perryman," Harry mused with his usual feigned innocence for his audience of Freddy Collins and Benny Green.

"And on the first night," Greg chimed in.

"I wonder who did it?" added Duster.

"What's a short sheet?" asked Benny, the sort of question you could expect from a greenhorn.

As was his patrol leader duty, Chucky patiently explained the process, trying his best not to laugh, and adding "Don't ever let me catch you doing that. You'll get expelled from camp, maybe from the troop."

The entire troop knew the drill. It was Scout's Honor time. Perryman couldn't wait until the next morning. He ordered all of the boys to line up in the dark on the Parade Grounds in front of the leaders' tent and swear to tell the truth under Scout's Honor. As the boys left the tent, Harry held up his pressed thumb and forefinger, reminding the other three of the Musketeer's Vow.

Perryman walked slowly down the entire line, shining his flashlight into each boy's face and demanding that they tell the truth. They all did. That is, all except the four Musketeers. Duster couldn't restrain his giggle when the light hit his face.

"What are you laughing about, Fertig?" demanded Perryman.

"Nothing, sir."

"Then wipe that stupid grin off your face. And you, Vincent. Why the smirk? What do you know about this?"

"I don't know anything, sir. I swear. Scout's Honor."

Perryman gave Harry a long look. Having had just about enough of Vincent's shenanigans, Putz considered him a prime suspect, but none of the Musketeers would budge and implicate a friend. The lineup produced nothing concrete that Putz could use.

After the boys retreated to their tents, Perryman ripped out the stitches and tried to replace his bedding, but the torn sheets didn't fully cooperate. As he lay in the dark, unable to sleep, an image flashed into his mind—the image of the four Hawks arriving late at the mess hall. He recalled Harry Vincent's smirk that night in the lineup, a repeated smirk he had grown to detest. Perryman promised himself that, sooner or later, he was going to wipe the smirk off Vincent's stupid face.

# CHAPTER 10

# PUTZ PERRYMAN

Putz Perryman woke up in the middle of the night knowing damn well that Vincent, the little shit, had short-sheeted him. He could spot shenanigans in Vincent's face: his puckered lips; his raised eyebrows; the arrogant slouch; and the way he flipped his right hip when he thought he had done something funny.

Perryman had seen too much of that attitude during Troop 64's weekly meetings. He should have unloaded on Vincent back then, especially when he was preparing the troop for its Indian dancing exhibition at this past spring's Boy Scout Roundup in the Municipal Auditorium.

With the entire Troop 64 formed in a large circle around him, Perryman had been demonstrating Native dance steps and teaching the boys how to make authentic Indian war whoops for their attack on Troop 38's wagon train at the Roundup. Having immersed himself in Indian lore for most of his thirty-four years, he wanted to make certain that the boys did it right. But their eyes kept wandering and grins kept emerging when the boys should have been intent and serious. Suddenly he turned around and spotted Vincent behind him, mocking Perryman's meticulous Indian choreography.

"What's with you, Vincent?" Perryman blurted. He wanted to say "you little fuck head," but the Boy Scouts frowned on such language, as did the board of directors of Brooklane Christian Church, where the troop met. So he merely called him Vincent.

"Nothing, sir," he answered obsequiously.

"I hope not," growled the adult leader, who went back to his teaching as boys around the room burst into laughter. If only he could get his hands around Vincent's scrawny neck and squeeze that protruding Adam's apple.

Perryman knew he should have dropped Vincent out of the Roundup, but he also knew he would have had a hell of a time doing it. He had suggested it to Scoutmaster Lloyd "Tux" Harrison, but Tux was such a softy. He always insisted on giving every boy a second or third or fourth chance. Perryman knew you had to be tough on them to build character, but Tux coddled the boys even when Bill knew he had it all wrong.

He could imagine Tux's wishy-washy excuses. *Are you really sure he was mimicking you? Maybe he was just having trouble learning the dance. All boys deserve another opportunity.* Blah, blah, blah. Perryman realized he couldn't start anything just then. He had too much work to do to get ready for the Roundup. But he hoped Vincent wouldn't cause any trouble during the show itself.

The night of the Roundup, Perryman gave a final pep talk to his Indians, now in breechcloths and war paint. "Make it loud and fierce, you guys. We've got a packed house tonight. I want you to scare the hell out of those pioneers. You're out to get their scalps!"

And for a couple of minutes they did sound sort of scary as they danced around the trapped wagon train and whooped it up Indian-style. Then Vincent went into his act, switching from Indian movements to bumps and grinds, like a strip teaser. Soon other boys joined him, rhythmically thrusting their pelvises in the direction of the pioneers, who began to laugh at their adversaries. Howls and applause from the audience encouraged even more of the boys to join the pelvis act, with the pioneers responding in kind.

Fortunately for Perryman, the whistle finally blew, signaling time for the boys to clear the floor so that the next set of troops could take over and erect their watch towers. As the Indians trooped out, they slapped Harry on the back, indicating their delight at his innovative leadership. Perryman could merely glare at the little fuck head who had desecrated his meticulous choreography. Too many boys had joined the parody. He was damned if he was going to do anything that might elevate Vincent into even more of a folk hero.

The next day Perryman demanded that Tux Harrison expel Harry Vincent from Troop 64. But Perryman knew his demands meant nothing when made to a wimp like Harrison, with his mushy insistence on giving his boys another chance, even a complete, unrepentant screw-up like Harry Vincent. In Vincent's case, this meant second, third, fourth, and fifth chances. After that Perryman quit counting.

As he tossed and turned, trying to ignore his shredded sheets, Perryman thought about the way that Vincent had negated his months of planning and ruined his big night at the Roundup. He knew this couldn't go on much longer. Someday, someone had to put the little prick in his place. Planning how to get even with Vincent helped Perryman finally get to sleep.

# CHAPTER 11

· · · · · · · · ·

# FLIPPER GREEN

Benny Green knew he had messed up. As he walked back to the Hawk tent late on Tuesday afternoon, he realized he should have switched patrols before they came down to Camp Matulia. He should have made that decision the moment, shortly after he had joined the Hawks, when Harry Vincent started calling him "Greenberg."

He wasn't exactly sure why his folks had changed their name a couple of years earlier. They merely said it would help, that it would make everything a little easier, and that he'd grow to understand. They weren't the only Jewish family that had changed its name. Willy Epstein's folks had become the Edmonds and the Rosenbaums had become the Rosses.

But Willy Epstein didn't have to put up with Harry Vincent. Willy had joined the Jewish troop that met at the synagogue, but Benny's folks told him they thought Troop 64 was a better fit and, besides, it was much closer to home. Benny actually liked the troop. It had lots of good activities and Tux Harrison seemed like a kind and thoughtful troop leader.

But being a Hawk was a different matter. He couldn't stand Harry Vincent riding him all the time. He hated it that Vincent kept calling him Greenberg and then named him "Flipper" because he had a small penis and no pubic hair, joking that Benny could only flip it rather than getting a good hold when he tried to masturbate.

Benny had talked to his folks about changing patrols, but

they said he should try to make a go of it. Something about not wanting to do anything that might cause others in the troop to think that Jews were troublemakers. He tried to explain to his folks what it was like being a Hawk, but he couldn't tell them about being called Flipper, so they didn't really understand.

Then there was the last camp-out in May, when the older guys had dipped his hand into a pot of warm water while he was sleeping, which made him piss in his sleeping bag. He didn't mind getting out of the smelly bag and sleeping on top of it, but he hated it when the four older guys started marching around his tent chanting, "Flipper pissed his sleeping bag! Flipper pissed his sleeping bag!"

After that, Benny decided to switch patrols no matter what his folks said. But he would wait until the end of summer so it wouldn't be a big deal at Camp Matulia. What a mistake! Now it had become a big deal, because Vincent had been riding him since they arrived. He couldn't spend eleven more nights in a tent with Vincent.

He thought Ed Marshall would understand. After all, he was the troop's volunteer counselor that summer. But instead all Marshall did was ask questions and say he would talk to Tux Harrison. He didn't seem to understand what it was like being called Greenberg when that wasn't his real name. Well, what could he expect from a goy like Marshall? In fact, all of the adult leaders were goyim. How could they understand?

And he sure couldn't explain about being called Flipper. That's not what you talked about to scout leaders. You could confide in them about some things, but not about the size of your pecker.

Benny looked into the Hawk tent to see if Harry Vincent were there. He couldn't handle one more "Greenberg" or "Flipper." Finding the tent empty, Benny lay down. Maybe he could talk to Vincent and ask him to lay off. If that didn't work, he could have it out with him.

Although Vincent was two years older, Benny had become a pretty good fighter for his age. He had sure whipped Allan Armstrong when they got into a fight during a kickball game at school. Bloodied his nose and made him cry. If he picked a fight with an older guy like Vincent and proved he could hold his own, he would show that he could stand up for himself and maybe the Hawks would stop riding him. A smile crossed Benny's face as he thought about blood flowing out of Vincent's nose and dripping into his mouth. What if he made Vincent beg him to stop?

Benny closed his eyes to enjoy the image of the supplicating bully. Suddenly his body stiffened and his fists clenched as he heard Vincent's loud voice getting nearer. He tensed up as he waited for the next "Greenberg."

· · · · · · · · ·

# CHAPTER 12

# FORESKIN FREDDY

In truth, Benny didn't have to worry about being singled out. Harry had already added Bill Perryman's scalp to his camp collection. And as much as Harry enjoyed having fun with Benny, he didn't have all that much time to waste on easy targets like the Jew boy. First, he had to take care of the other younger scout in the Hawk tent, Freddy Collins.

Freddy knew he should have been more alert. Why would Harry Vincent, who had ridden him unmercifully about his foreskin since he joined the patrol, suddenly ask him to be his partner at the pool that Tuesday afternoon? Maybe Freddy was hoping that Harry had undergone a change of heart and had decided to be friends. Maybe Harry had finally realized that he shouldn't be acting that way just because Freddy's parents had decided not to have him circumcised.

Freddy wasn't the only boy with a foreskin. Most of his friends who attended St. Matthew's Parochial School with him had foreskins, too. That was the Catholic way. Protestants and Jews got circumcised, although he wasn't sure why Catholics didn't.

That wasn't something he could discuss with his parents, but it sure made a difference in a troop with so few Catholics. He could tell by the stares from other scouts when he changed clothes or had to pee. Those were times when he wished he had joined a Catholic troop.

But now Harry had asked him to be his pool buddy. He even called him Freddy, not "Foreskin Freddy," which came as a real relief. Maybe he had passed the greenhorn test. Anxious to please the older Hawk, Freddy headed down to the pool with his new friend.

Camp Matulia had a strict formal swimming pool ritual, which included something they called "buddy check." First, all boys had to use the communal shower, both entering and leaving the pool. Fortunately for Freddy, boys wore their bathing suits while showering. Then they jumped into the pool in pairs, holding hands, so lifeguards could make certain every scout had a buddy.

After the boys jumped into the pool, lifeguards would periodically blow a whistle and shout "buddy check," at which point each pair of boys would clench hands—one hand each—and lift them high to show that both buddies were OK. Once the lifeguards had ascertained that all buddy pairs were accounted for—meaning no stray boys floundering somewhere under water—the whistle would blow again and swimming would resume. The tedious ritual helped Camp Matulia maintain its fine pool safety record.

There were, however, unofficial rituals that had developed informally among the boys but had not been ordained by camp leaders, things like underwater crotch-grabbing and shower room depantsing. Depantsing consisted of slipping up behind an unsuspecting swimmer, hooking your fingers into the top of his trunks, and quickly yanking them down while shouting to everyone else to get a good look at the newly exposed victim.

Basking in what he hoped had become a *real* friendship—or at least enjoying the welcome respite from being called Foreskin Freddy—the young Catholic was caught completely off guard. The opening shower went fine, and Harry seemed genuinely friendly as they swam, joked, and raised their clenched hands during buddy check. Freddy joyfully began his departure shower prior to heading back to the Hawk tent.

Suddenly he felt Vincent's thumbs hooking the back of his waistband and his trunks being pulled down almost to his knees, accompanied by Harry shouting, "Look at Foreskin Freddy! Look at Foreskin Freddy!" All eyes—at least it seemed that way to Freddy—focused on his crotch.

Then the chorus went up, "Freddy, Freddy, Freddy," the traditional naming chant for anyone caught by a depantsing. Freddy grabbed his trunks to pull them up, but Vincent's hand held them down for what seemed like minutes. Finally letting go, Vincent went into his standard routine.

"Come on, Freddy, it's a joke. Just a plain old foreskin joke. It's part of your Matulia initiation."

More laughter. Although feeling every eye on him, Freddy mustered a smile.

"Sure. Just a joke."

Like hell it was just a joke. Freddy was sick and tired of being just a joke. Damn tired of being a Catholic joke and having to answer dumb questions like why they didn't eat meat on Fridays or why priests couldn't get married or why Catholics didn't wear rubbers when they did it or did he have to tell the priest about masturbating when he went to confession? Above all, why didn't they get circumcised like normal boys and wasn't it yucky having all that extra meat hanging down and how did he keep his big old pecker clean?

Although he had been patient about answering those dumb questions, the relentless process was wearing him out. He had even talked to Benny Green to try to understand how he put up with kidding, especially from Harry Vincent. Maybe they both ought to change patrols, or maybe he just ought to change troops, since Vincent had made certain that everyone in Troop 64 thought of him as "Foreskin Freddy."

Damn, if he had just been more alert. He had been warned about crotch-grabbing in the pool and depantsing in the shower, but he had been so distracted by Vincent's invitation to be his pool buddy. This would be the last time that Vincent would ever surprise him. Now it was his turn to catch Vincent off guard and let him have it good.

As they walked back to the troop compound, Vincent continued to bask in the somewhat-imagined adulation for his successful depantsing of Foreskin Freddy. He didn't seem to notice how angry Freddy had become.

# CHAPTER 13

# ADULT LEADERS

Some might find it strange that the adult leaders didn't crack down on such bullying. Quite the contrary, they looked upon these shenanigans as a normal part—maybe even an important part—of camp ritual. After all, boys will be boys. If you want them to develop into men, real men, you've got to let them learn to fend for themselves, one of the things that made Boy Scouts different from Girl Scouts.

There were plenty of adult leaders who could have intervened if they really wanted to. First the general camp leadership who stayed there all summer, under the firm and boisterous direction of Rocky Reynolds. The professional staff made the whole camp function in a way that had become a national model, a place frequently visited and viewed with awe by scout leaders from around the country. This included leaders from much bigger cities that actually had major league baseball teams, not minor league teams like the Kaioga City Blazers.

Each troop compound had its own team of adult volunteers, housed together in a leadership tent. In the summer of 1948, Troop 64 had three adult leaders, led by troop Scoutmaster Harrison, who spent every summer at Camp Matulia with his boys. This was very impressive, because not all scoutmasters were willing to sacrifice two weeks of their precious vacation time to rough it at Matulia. Although friendly and thoughtful, Tux Harrison had a reserved, somewhat stiff, personal style, which didn't seem to fit with the fact that he had become a successful life insurance agent. The boys seemed to respect his consideration and fairness.

Tux had reservations about that summer's leadership team: first-timer Ed Marshall, who lacked wilderness experience, and camp veteran Bill Perryman, who could be a real pain in the ass. Tux hoped he could get them to work together, particularly since he had built Troop 64 into a smooth-running operation that didn't require any particular initiative from his associates.

Edward Marshall still wasn't sure why he had agreed to come down that summer to be troop counselor. He liked working with boys, but as he lay awake that first night listening to Perryman bitch about his torn sheets, Marshall realized that he was already counting the days until he could return to civilization.

Tux had made it clear that Ed's main role was to help boys with personal problems. Ed hoped that such counseling would provide him with a welcome respite from his immersion in facts and figures as an electrical engineer back in Kaioga City. He enjoyed sitting down and talking boys through their problems, although he had to admit he wasn't sure how to deal with overly sensitive kids like Benny Green, Jews who got upset just because they didn't want to be referred to by their real Jewish names.

Tux had to keep a closer eye on lanky, pompous Bill Perryman, who spent two weeks every summer at Camp Matulia, taking a break from his popular bakery loaded with pastries he designed and decorated. Perryman specialized in Indian lore, particularly Indian dancing. He studied it intensively and taught it with ferocity, hoping to transmit his love for all things Indian. Each night after campfire he would gather his small band of disciples for a brief session on the Parade Grounds, where they gazed at constellations and listened to Perryman relate Indian myths about their tribal origins.

Tux's main challenge was to make certain that the three of them worked like a team, each taking care of his designated specialty but also coming together to make crucial decisions, deal with major problems, and lead the boys in adventures such as nature hikes. Of course, all three had to share comradeship in the never-ending war against ticks, which had to be extracted from boys' scrota by applying warm matches to the rumps of the little critters so they would back out on their own. No yanking, as that might leave the head in the scrotum and force them to call a doctor, who would have to scrape it out.

There may have been more ticks than rocks at Camp Matulia. That's why, every few nights, the adult leaders would shout "tick inspection." Then all the boys were supposed to drop their pants and check each other's nuts, amid predictable laughter and jokes, directed mainly at kids who had the misfortune of not having pubic hair or not being circumcised, like Foreskin Freddy.

But this summer differed from previous years because the adult leaders were distracted by something even more critical—the 1948 presidential election. The discovery of Harry Vincent's body came at a particularly inopportune time, since it competed with the adult leaders' celebration about the forthcoming election of New York Governor Thomas Dewey as the next President of the United States.

Actually, they merely celebrated Dewey's nomination at the June 1948 Republican National Convention, which they listened to via radio with universal satisfaction. However, his election in November was a given since everybody knew—Tux certainly knew—that nobody in his right mind would vote for his Democratic opponent, current President Harry Truman, the local joke from nearby Independence, Missouri. After all, Truman had only become President by a fluke, taking over because the real president, Franklin D. Roosevelt, had died in 1945 shortly after being inaugurated for his fourth term.

Moreover, as one of the adult leaders put it, the only good thing Truman had ever done was drop the big one—make that two big ones—on the Japs to end World War II. Now he was trying to do stupid things like desegregating the military by forcing Negroes into white units, where they obviously didn't belong. This meant sharing barracks, pools, and for God's sake, showers. Hadn't Truman learned anything from the Scouts, who would never consider doing something that ridiculous?

But before they could elect Dewey, the Troop 64 leaders had to deal with something more at hand. That evening, that very Wednesday evening, somebody had set off a lolly trap in Lola's six-holer. The election of Tom Dewey would have to wait.

# CHAPTER 14

# LOLLY TRAP

A lolly trap didn't fall into the acceptable "boys-will-be-boys" category with stuff like depantsing. Adult leaders considered lolly traps to be a serious affront to the Camp Matulia moral code. It could even result in a boy being expelled from camp, maybe even from the Scouts.

Lolly traps were as simple as they were lethal. In fact, they were lethal because they were so simple. Anybody who could tie a knot could set a lolly trap. Since knot-tying ranked as a prime Boy Scout skill, this meant that every scout became a potential outhouse terrorist.

First you needed to choose the proper setting. Troop 64's ramshackle six-hole outhouse, Lola's Lolly, passed muster because of its location. Virtually isolated at the bottom of a densely forested hill that sloped away from the troop compound, Lola's Lolly seldom basked in moonlight. While boys took different routes to reach the outhouse by clambering down through the forest, it had one "official" access route, a steep, slippery, pebble-covered, Z-shaped gantlet known popularly as the "lolly path." Harry Vincent's dead body would be discovered on that path the following evening.

The lolly and, therefore, the path leading down to it got lots of use, at least from most of the scouts and leaders. "Most" being the operative word, because some scouts were so disgusted by the six-holer that they swore never to use it. Legend has it that a few scouts actually made it through the entire two weeks without ever taking a crap but, mind you, that claim has never been empirically documented.

Most scouts just tried to minimize their use of Lola's Lolly. After all, it was not a resort destination. Really just a small unlit wooden shed with some openings high on the walls to provide daylight visibility. At night, flashlights were advisable.

The shed contained one piece of furniture: a five-foot-wide, twelve-foot-long rotting wooden board containing two parallel sets of three butt-shaped holes. The individual holes were covered by equally noxious rotting wooden lids. Lolly etiquette called for boys to lower the lids when they had completed their business, a practice often ignored in their haste to escape the penetrating odor.

The board stretched the length of the shed, consuming about two-thirds of the space. Down the center of the board ran a thin, ten-inch-high beam, which marginally separated the two sides of the six-holed plank. Presumably this center beam provided a backboard against which boys could lean while taking their turn. However, since most boys raced in and out of the lolly while trying to hold their breath, particularly when all six holes were in use, they didn't usually avail themselves of that luxury.

Of course, this description begs the question: Where did the boys' collective refuse go? The answer was as direct as it was disgusting, at least to city boys accustomed to private bathrooms and flush toilets. Deep beneath the plank lay a huge pit into which everything fell. Scouts disagreed about the distance from the holes to the pit and sometimes placed bets on its depth. However, because nobody would volunteer to climb into the pit to get an accurate measurement, such disagreements were never definitively answered.

The camp staff assured the boys that the refuse continuously soaked into the earth, a less-than-convincing argument. On top of that, the camp maintenance team regularly dumped lye into the pit to accelerate the process. However, for most scouts, this official information did not make lolly visits more desirable, particularly when all six holes were active and you occasionally became the recipient of your neighbor's splashes.

While the lolly was a nightmare, lolly traps could be veritable works of art. Creating one was actually pretty easy, a form of artistic expression passed down over the decades, taught to greenhorns by camp veterans. First, you got a big rock and a short, stout piece of rope. Then you tied one end of the rope firmly around the rock and made a strong, solid, bulging knot at the other end.

Around dusk, just before the unlit outhouse became bathed in darkness, you waited near the lolly, hoping it would become vacated. Then you would slip quietly into the outhouse, raise one of the seat covers, lower the rock into the abyss, and close the cover so that only the knot was showing. The entire homemade rock weapon would be secured by wedging the lowered toilet cover snugly against the protruding knot.

Then all you had to do was wait. Sooner or later, an unsuspecting scout—better yet, an adult leader—would come along. He would nonchalantly lift the lid, thereby releasing the knot and causing the rock to plummet directly into the pool of human waste.

With some luck, this resulted in a geyser that ascended until it struck whatever happened to be resting above, hopefully the exposed butts of scouts sitting on adjacent holes. In the best of all possible worlds, all of the other toilet holes would be occupied, meaning five easy targets. Sometimes the assailant would manage a bonus strike, the face of the insufficiently aware scout who opened the cover and failed to jump back from the resulting geyser.

Now in his third summer at Matulia, Hawk Patrol leader Chucky Karlson qualified as a camp veteran. Well-versed in lolly lore, he regularly carried a flashlight to spot lolly traps. But that dark Wednesday evening, Chucky was distracted. In his first camp session as patrol leader, he hadn't been doing well. He was fumbling in his merit badge classes and had found supervising his tent to be an unexpected chore, particularly since Harry Vincent started in on him with his "Merona boy" crap every time he asked Harry to cooperate. In moments like that, Chucky regressed into his sense of being a hick town outsider, even among the Musketeers.

Whatever the reason, a distracted Chucky didn't check things out when he entered the lolly. With five of the holes taken, he lifted the sixth and final cover, felt the jerk as the rope slipped, heard the splash, and felt the spray. It was a rare lolly trap grand slam: five bare butts and a face.

Shouts echoed throughout the lolly. Shouts of anguish over wet butts merged with shouts of anger directed at Karlson for his negligence. Worse yet, getting caught in a facial meant Chucky would now be saddled with the nickname earned by all scouts who made such a blunder: Shit-Face. He could wash off the drippings, but there was no way to avoid the ribbing he would get for the rest of the session and for who knows how long after they got back to Kaioga City.

It would have been the perfect crime if not for Harry Vincent's big mouth. He had bragged that he was going to set a lolly trap and, after he learned of his success, he boasted about his triumph. He also couldn't restrain himself from snickering "Hi, Shit-Face" when he saw Karlson that night at the campfire, all the confirmation that the already furious Chucky needed.

The unofficial camp code of honor—clearly not the *official* one—proclaimed that you didn't rat on others who succeeded in pulling off a lolly trap, even if you were a victim. So nobody reported Harry to the adult leaders. Oh, the leaders heard about the event, but they knew that the camp honor code made it very unlikely they would ever discover the culprit. However, they had their suspicions. Bill Perryman certainly did. If only Tux Harrison had listened to him and expelled that little creep Vincent after the Scout Roundup fiasco.

But fretting about the Scout Roundup or carping about short sheeting, depantsing, or lolly traps evaporated the next day when, shortly after dusk, Terry Fleener stumbled over Harry Vincent's lifeless body flopped across the lolly path, about halfway down to the outhouse.

· · · · · · · · ·

# CHAPTER 15

# TUX HARRISON

When Tux Harrison decided to dedicate himself to scouting, he hadn't figured that becoming scoutmaster might someday mean he would be dealing with a boy's death. He loved how scouting could help boys develop into men, so he didn't consider it a sacrifice to spend every Wednesday night at Brooklane Christian Church for troop meetings and two weeks every summer at Camp Matulia, even though it meant a shorter vacation with his own family.

In his professional life, Tux had lots of experience with death, since he had to work with families of the deceased to whom he had sold life insurance policies. But this was different. He had never grappled with a death on his own camp watch.

Tux faced numerous challenges. Having to explain to the Vincents, by phone, what had happened to their son. Helping with arrangements for sending Harry's body to the mortuary in Kaioga City. Getting special permission for the Vincents to come to camp on Saturday, not the normal Visitors' Sunday, to pick up Harry's belongings once the sheriff gave his OK. Being questioned by the sheriff and the coroner. Trying to comfort boys who broke down crying and pleaded to go home. Having to deal with his two unpredictable adult associates: temperamental Bill Perryman, whose actions had become increasingly annoying since being short-sheeted; and the normally calm and cerebral Ed Marshall, who now seemed to have trouble making even small decisions.

Tux determined that the only way to make it through this crisis was by maintaining complete control of himself, not allowing himself to react emotionally, even if this meant being robotically methodical, taking things one step at a time. One at a time. One at a time. Focus on the task at hand. Solve that problem. Prepare for the unexpected.

He spent much of the Friday morning after Harry's death with Camp Director Rocky Reynolds and Sheriff Lester Jones, who kept admonishing him with the increasingly irritating rejoinder, "Just call me 'Pug.' Plain old Pug. 'Ug' with a 'P.'" Pug inspected the scene of the accident with nauseating slowness, pacing up and down the lolly path and carefully perusing the tree-studded section where the body had been found.

The sheriff studied what seemed like every detail of the path's enormous, inverted Z. The path first dropped straight down from the compound, then zigged sharply but less steeply to the left through a grove of trees, and finally zagged just as sharply down to the right, ending at Lola's Lolly. Harry's body had been discovered on the middle zig section, where trees partially obscured a clear vision from either the compound or the lolly. The obscurity of that section helped convince Pug that Harry could have fallen without being seen. Nevertheless, he told Tux that he would come back that afternoon and maybe Saturday morning for more questioning.

Aching with the tension of having to spend most of the morning with the sheriff, Tux lay down and closed his eyes. But not for long. He was soon awakened by a runner from Rocky Reynolds, saying the camp director had to see him right away.

Tux admired and, at times, envied Reynolds' confident, outgoing manner, even though Rocky's penchant for bellowing sometimes proved difficult for the reserved Troop 64 leader. But the boys all loved Reynolds' swagger, his constant joking, and especially the way he could get hundreds of boys to sing rousing, male-bonding ditties in the mess hall or at general campfires. When Tux reached the director's cabin, Reynolds seemed anxious to get down to business.

"Tux, we've got to be real careful. The sheriff asked me some tough questions. And now the *Kaioga City Tribune* wants more information for its story and obituary. Fortunately, The Boss knows lots of people at the *Tribune.* He's been talking to them all morning, so we shouldn't come out looking too bad. But we've got to be careful when the newspaper starts its interviewing. A boy's death doesn't make us look very good in print."

"The Boss told me that the *Tribune's* planning three stories. A short one about Vincent's death in this afternoon's paper. An obituary tomorrow. And later maybe a nice little feature story about the Vincent kid. You know, stuff about how he enjoyed camp and how much the other boys liked him. Of course, what your adult leaders remember about him, how great he was to work with, how much he contributed to Troop 64. By the way, how well did you know Vincent?"

Tux thought about the Boy Scout Roundup and Perryman's reaction to the short sheeting, as well as rumors about Vincent's involvement in depantsing and the lolly trap. He looked blankly at Reynolds.

"I knew him…like I know all the boys. Well, but not unusually well. Nothing special to say."

"That's probably good, Tux. Too special and we get too much attention. So here's the deal. We'll be getting a call from the *Tribune* in a few minutes. Don't say too much. Maybe something a little bit personal about him. The Boss will be checking on the story from his end. Oh, should we have one of your other leaders come up for the call? Maybe Ed Marshall?"

Tux had to answer carefully. Slowly shaking his head, he spoke softly and seriously. "No, it's probably best if I handle it. I'll come up with something."

Actually, Tux didn't have to do much talking. Rocky did

most of the jabbering with the *Tribune* reporter. Rocky always did most of the talking and joking and singing. That's why he had become camp director, while Tux remained the dependable troop leader.

When his turn came, Tux kept it simple. "Harry Vincent was a very popular scout. The other boys liked him. The adult leaders thought very highly of him. We'll all miss him."

Rocky watched uneasily, poised to grab the phone if the wrong words seemed about to come out. When Tux handed the phone back to him, Rocky took a deep breath.

"Anything more? Good. We'll look forward to the story," he said as he hung up. "Nice job, Tux. One down, one to go."

"One to go?"

"Yeah, the feature story. After the obit, the *Tribune's* going to do the little feature story I told you about. It will be about Vincent and, of course, the camp. Let the parents know we run a safe, happy place. Take good care of their boys."

"Oh."

"I'm depending on you to make sure things are in order when the reporter gets here. You probably ought to talk to Marshall and Perryman. Make sure they're with the agenda. We can't afford any slip-ups."

"Certainly."

"And the other boys in his patrol?"

"The Hawks?"

"Maybe you ought to talk to them before the reporter gets down here. You know, make certain they know what to say. What I mean is, what they shouldn't say. It's up to you to make sure they don't say anything…you know."

"Anything that makes us appear negligent."

"Yeah, sort of. And anything about the Vincent kid that might…you know."

"That might look bad in the paper."

Reynolds smiled. "You've got it, Tux. I'm counting on you to take care of things with your team."

The two adversaries stared silently at each other. Tux could tell there was something else.

"Tux, the sheriff's coming back this afternoon. Wants to question more people...including your two adult leaders."

Tux was afraid of where this was going, but he couldn't do anything to head it off.

"Tux, I've heard rumors about stuff between Bill Perryman and the Vincent kid."

"Yes, Rocky, there's been stuff. Do you want me to tell you about it?"

"No, Tux. Keep it to yourself. And tell that hot-head Perryman to keep it to himself, too. This isn't the time to start blabbing about personal animosities. We've got to think of the scouts."

"Of course."

"And while we're at it, Tux, is there anything going on in the Hawk Patrol that we need to worry about? Now don't tell me. I don't want to know. Just make sure the Hawks are all part of the team."

"Rocky, they're boys."

"I know damn well they're boys. That's why I'm worried. They've got to act like men, realize what's important, the reputation of the Scouts. That's up to you, completely up to you. You're their scoutmaster. I'm counting on you. The Boss is counting on you. Everyone's counting on you." Reynolds' rat-a-tatting stopped, as he stared in silence at Harrison. Then came the threat. "Got it, Tux?"

Tux paused and gathered himself. "Got it, Rocky."

*Is this why I became a scout leader?* Tux moped, as he trudged back to the troop site. *Perryman? The Hawks? Make sure. Everyone's counting on you. Everyone's watching you. Everyone's judging you.* Tux looked down at the fingers of his right hand. He'd be using plenty of Scout's Honors in the next few days. He'd have to.

For some reason, Tux began smiling as he imagined telling Perryman to pledge on Scout's Honor that he would only say nice things about Harry Vincent. He chuckled as he thought about the reporter asking Perryman whether Vincent was a good Indian dancer. *Stop it, Tux. This is serious business.* But he almost chuckled again.

# CHAPTER 16

# MARCHING ORDERS

Tux decided to talk to Perryman and Marshall at the same time. If he talked to them alone, Perryman would feel free to throw one of his fits. That's not what he needed right now. Maybe having greenhorn Ed Marshall around would help calm things down, although Ed had gone into sort of a trance since Harry Vincent's death.

Before they headed to the mess hall for lunch, Tux told the two of them to stick around after the meal. He needed to talk to them privately. Their tent was too exposed. As the boys headed back to the compound after lunch, the three men strolled down the overlook trail toward the general council ring.

"Look, you guys, I just had a long talk with Rocky Reynolds. A serious talk. He's very worried about how the camp is going to look when this is all over. After the sheriff's through with his investigation, the *Tribune's* probably going to send a reporter down to do a feature story on Harry Vincent. It's got to be a positive story. Reynolds doesn't want anything said about Vincent that might make the Scouts look bad."

Perryman stopped and glared at Tux. "Are you saying Reynolds wants us to lie?"

"I didn't say that, Bill," Tux snapped. "I merely explained that Rocky doesn't want us to say anything that makes the Scouts look bad."

As Perryman planned his next gambit, Marshall computed Tux's statement. "What you're telling us is that we shouldn't volunteer much, right? Just stick to the basic facts. No rumors or gossip."

Tux looked at Marshall. "Just be very, very careful what you say and focus on how your answers could make the Scouts look, make the troop look...make us look...if they got into print."

By now Perryman was ready to rise to the challenge.

"Let me get this straight, Tux. You're saying that if the reporter asks me about Vincent, like what kind of a scout he was, I'm supposed to feed him a bunch of crap about that little prick? Make him seem like some sort of saint?"

Tux decided to play his trump card. "It's not just Rocky. It's orders from The Boss. Andy Norcutt's working the Kaioga City end of things. That's why he's the Scout Leader. That's why he spends so much time schmoozing with the press and the big-money donors. He's great at that kind of stuff. It's up to us to hold up our part of the bargain."

"What fucking bargain, Tux? I didn't make any bargain to lie about little shit-asses who never should have been in the Scouts in the first place, screw-ups who would have been bounced if you..."

"Look, Bill," Tux interrupted with growing irritation. "This comes from the top. It comes directly from The Boss, maybe from National. There's much more at stake than personal grievances."

Perryman knew he was cornered. He could tell Tux to get lost, that he wasn't about to bow down to loud-mouth Rocky Reynolds, who never really appreciated important stuff like making sure that the boys did their Indian dancing in a truly authentic manner. That son-of-a-bitch camp director would be perfectly happy if they just whooped and hollered like savages.

But The Boss was different. Andy Norcutt, head of the Boy Scouts in Kaioga City, had become one of the biggest names in scouting nationally, almost a legend for the way he had built the local program, the envy of leaders all around the country. Crossing him would be a one-way, fast-track ticket out of scouting.

A veteran salesman, Tux could spot when he had the upper hand in negotiations, so he took advantage of his momentary edge. "Then there's something else. We've got to make certain the Hawks don't mess things up either. We need to be careful not to interfere with the sheriff's investigation, but as soon as he finishes, we've got to meet with them and prep them for their interviews with the *Tribune*."

Tux hadn't planned this final interjection. In fact, he had been considering meeting with the Hawks alone without hot-head Perryman and slow-talking newcomer Marshall. But now he realized he didn't feel like shouldering the entire responsibility. He wasn't going to be Rocky Reynolds' fall guy. He'd rather include Bill and Ed as co-conspirators. No, no, no! This was no conspiracy. They were just trying to do their duty to make certain the boys didn't say anything that might turn this unfortunate incident into a scandal.

Ed Marshall nodded mechanically, as if unable to grasp the entrapping web being spun. Bill Perryman grasped it all too well. He was not only being forced to lie about that little punk Vincent, but he was also being asked to help scare the Hawks into doing the same thing.

"Are we all on board?" asked Tux, his eyes darting back and forth between Perryman and Marshall, who kept nodding like a metronome. "How about you, Bill?" Tux probed. Furious at Tux for trapping him and furious at himself for letting it happen, Perryman surrendered. "Sure."

Tux felt proud of himself for pulling this off. Maybe he was a leader, after all. Smiling gently—he hoped not smugly—he added, "We ought to be getting back to the compound. Sheriff Jones is likely to be showing up anytime."

# CHAPTER 17

# PUG JONES

Pug Jones chomped down on his heavily breaded, cream-sauce-buried pork tenderloin and mused about what fun he was going to have that afternoon. The case was pretty much closed, since Mike Maldeth, the country coroner, had figured it out quickly. The evidence was clear enough that even a second-rater like Maldeth could get it right.

It had been turning dark, rapidly. The Vincent kid must have been careless, either walking too fast or not putting his feet down firmly as you had to do on those slippery hillsides. A city boy mistake. His heels must have slid out from under him, sending him crashing down on his back, his skull hitting a rock. A freak accident, sure, but freak accidents do happen.

Pug could probably close the case right now after his morning visit to the camp, but he decided to have fun with the city crowd, shake them up some more. That was one of the pleasures of being sheriff of Green River County. Enough action, but not too much, so you didn't have to rush things.

His family liked it here, too. His oldest son was making noises about going away to college and maybe settling in the big city. That was OK. Kids move on. For old Pug, though, Green River County was just fine. Born here, die here. Plenty of hunting and fishing. Be a good family man. What more could you ask?

Of course, get a little ass on the side from young clerks and waitresses who thought old Pug's badge made him hot stuff.

Obviously he usually avoided high school girls, although that redhead with the big blue eyes and huge tits could have gotten him into real trouble. It certainly wasn't his fault she looked so much older. Anyway, she's married now and probably won't blab to her husband that he's only getting seconds.

Pug's biggest problem was Camp Matulia. Well, not the camp itself, which ran pretty well. It was the big city parents who came down on Visitors' Sundays to make sure their spoiled little babies were doing OK.

So when summertime came around and those locusts started swarming down from Kaioga City, Pug and his deputies didn't have as much time to deal with local stuff like drunks and fights between gangs of farm kids from rival schools. Instead he made sure his deputies kept their eyes open for Kaioga City reckless drivers who didn't seem to give a damn when they whipped through the area on their way to Camp Matulia. His boys always managed to slap plenty of speeding tickets on them, which the deputies liked because they got a kick out of watching those city drivers complain and try to talk their way out of fines, always failing, hilariously. Especially the ones who would go into their "don't you know who I am" routines, as if that meant anything to him and his boys.

Mondays would always be good times for jokes in the office. Jokes about the big city people with their big city words, their big city accents, and their big city attitudes. All of them talking fast rather than relaxing and taking their time like Green River folks.

Then there were stories about the horny little scouts, brought home mainly by Hexterville women who worked in the camp mess hall or helped the doctor at the health lodge. Some of the adult leaders were even worse, pawing every woman in sight as if coming from Kaioga City gave them special rights.

The Boss was OK. He ran a mighty tight ship. In fact, Pug considered him to be a pretty good dude. Andy Norcutt often stopped off at the county office to chew the fat with Pug and some of the other Hexterville top dogs. He always sent Pug a Christmas card and even took him out for lunch now and then. That wiry little son of a bitch knows how to take care of his friends.

Pug knew Norcutt wasn't doing all this because he loved them, since every once in a while The Boss would call in a favor, usually to try to take care of some camp incident, like an adult leader or an older scout making a pass at one of the cooks. Favors were OK with Pug. He'd do right by The Boss as long as he didn't ask for too much or try to get them to drop a speeding ticket, which he never did. The Boss reciprocated by letting Green River kids use the camp at the end of summer after Kaioga City was through with it. Both of Pug's boys had gone there.

The Boss also made sure that things ran as smoothly as possible at camp. The important thing was taking great care about what troops came down together for each session. Pug figured The Boss didn't have to do this personally, since Kaioga City had a natural social separation with a long tradition.

The North End troops, mainly Italians and Irish, came for one session or maybe two. Then the Westside, meaning poor whites and a few Mexicans, always came for the last session, when the place was getting a bit rundown, especially the swimming pool.

Of course, no problem with Negroes. The Kaioga City Council had built them their own little camp just south of the city. It didn't have all the goodies of Matulia, but so what? At least they had a pool. What more could they ask?

But most Matulia kids were middle class, mainly from south Kaioga City. Some even lived in those mansions over by the

Missouri-Kansas state line. So many of them came that they filled up at least three sessions, usually early in the summer when the camp was still fresh.

On his infrequent visits to Kaioga City, Pug enjoyed driving up and down Western Boulevard, with its broad grass islands separating the northbound and southbound traffic, some islands so long and wide you could play football on them. He gawked at the mansions facing Western. Who in the hell needed a house that big?

Of course there were more problems at Matulia when the southsiders were there. That's when he heard stories about kids demanding this or demanding that or scouts breaking down in the health lodge and crying that they wanted to go home to Mommy. So it made sense that the first fatality in Camp Matulia history occurred when the spoiled brats from south Kaioga City were there.

Mike Maldeth had pointed out a few things he couldn't fully explain. Nothing major, just little stuff like a bump on Vincent's forehead. Probably hit his head on a branch earlier that day or done some other stupid city boy thing. But what if Pug made it into something bigger, just for a few hours? What if he began asking questions about the bump, hinting that maybe someone hit him and knocked him down? He couldn't wait to see their scaredy-cat faces when they realized they might be suspects in a killing.

Pug swallowed the last piece of his pork tenderloin and strapped on his revolver. This was going to be a fun afternoon.

. . . . . . . . .

# CHAPTER 18

# INTERVIEWS

$P$ug decided to start with the Troop 64 adult leaders. He had already gotten all he could from that arrogant camp director Rocky Reynolds, who always put on a southern Missouri accent to try to hide his city talk. Who in hell did he think he was fooling? Lloyd Harrison, the Troop 64 scoutmaster, hadn't been much help, although he did walk Pug up and down the path heading to the lolly so he could see where Harry Vincent had died.

Pug and his deputy had spent some of the morning looking around that path for evidence but couldn't find much of value. They could have taken fingerprints at the scene, but of what? Even if Harry had been hit by a something like a rock, which Pug considered highly unlikely, which rock? There were hundreds of them on the hill around the lolly path. Moreover, if someone *had* hit him, that someone could have thrown the rock way down the hill. Pug decided that this needle-in-a-haystack probing wasn't worth the effort, especially given Coroner Maldeth's conclusion of accidental death.

As he drove the long, winding gravel road from the potted two-lane county highway into Camp Matulia, Pug smiled as he laid out the line of questioning he would follow with the troop's adult leaders, starting with the way they found the body. He'd get them off-balance from the start, asking about the red bump on Harry's forehead.

The questioning went even better than Pug had imagined, meaning the adult leaders seemed more perplexed with every question. He loved watching the city folks squirm. *If Harry died from hitting the back of his head on a rock when he fell, how do you explain that bump on his forehead? Oh, so now you're suggesting that someone may have discovered Harry lying on his face, turned him over, gotten scared, and then run off? What about a simpler explanation: Maybe someone hit Harry on the forehead with something like a rock and knocked him down. If so, who? Did anybody in your troop have a grudge against Vincent?* Pug chuckled as he watched the adult leaders wrestle with that one.

*Hm, so you think Vincent may have fallen, hit the back of his head, and then bounced or rolled over on his face, where he got the bump? Then how come he ended up on his back? Oh, so now you're suggesting he may have fallen down face first, bumped his forehead, and then rolled over on his back? That's a likely scenario! You're forgetting about the severe dent in the back of his head, like from a long fall. Or are you saying he fell down face first, hit his forehead, stood up, and then fell back down again on his back?*

*Did any of you see Harry Vincent fall? Or get hit? Why not? Aren't you guys supposed to be supervising what goes on with your troop? Who was the last one of you to see him?*

*Oh, and while we're at it, let's talk about motive. Did Vincent have any enemies? How about you three?* Pug grinned. They weren't expecting that one. He loved the shocked looks on their arrogant big city faces when he made it seem as if they might be murder suspects.

Now the adult leaders seemed truly flustered, especially when he got to the part about Harry having enemies. It was all Pug could do to keep from laughing out loud at their discomfort. The way they started stammering, he half expected them to blurt out their own confessions of first-degree murder. He probably should have made it clear that they weren't really suspects but, what the hell, let them stew in it for a night before he came back tomorrow and told them the investigation was closed.

Leaving the adult leaders to fret, Pug headed for the Hawk tent. The boys were at their merit badge classes, so Pug wandered around for a while. Damn, Camp Matulia was gorgeous. No wonder he loved the area so much. These city kids didn't realize how lucky they were, getting to spend two weeks at Matulia. Hell, they were probably counting the days until they got back to their well-trimmed parks, sanitized burger joints, Sunday afternoon triple-feature movies, and, of course, their mommies. Let them have it. He'd take Green River anytime.

It was getting late when the boys returned from their afternoon classes to get ready for a dip in the pool. But that would have to wait. Pug decided to interview all of the Hawks at the same time. He didn't feel like going through the routine five times since there probably wasn't much more to learn anyway.

Pug squatted on Harry Vincent's metal cot and looked at the boys, one at a time, making direct, piercing eye contact. "OK, boys, I would like each of you to tell me about the last time— the very last time—you saw Harry Vincent alive."

Their testimonies came out in jerks and snorts. They all had been with him at dinner at the mess hall. After dinner, some had gone to the softball game against Troop 30. Benny Green had talked to him in the tent. The last one to see him seemed to be Chucky Karlson, who described conversing with Vincent near the top of the lolly path just before he started his fateful descent. "Then Harry headed down toward the lolly and Trent Georgis of the Rabbit Patrol came up to talk to me. That's the last I saw of Harry until they found him dead. Check with Trent. He'll tell you that's what happened. I swear."

"Don't worry, Mr. Karlson. I will definitely check with— what's his name? Georgis?" Pug said slowly, while writing down the name and silently cursing the fact that he'd have to do another meaningless interview.

By now Pug had had his fill of fun. He was intent on finishing the Hawk interview and dealing with the Georgis kid so he could go home. In fact, he was so intent that he almost forgot his "enemies" question.

"One other thing. Do you know anyone who might have had a grudge against Vincent?" After giving them a few seconds to mull it over, Pug added, "Did any of you have anything against him?"

Chucky jumped in. "No. None of us did. I don't know anyone who did. Harry was our friend." The rest of them nodded silently.

Pug looked slowly from face to face. He knew damn well they were hiding something, but so what? Everybody has grudges, but that doesn't mean you go out and kill somebody. Anyway, the case was closed. Maldeth had already determined accidental death. If one of the boys started blabbing about some grievance against Vincent, where would it stop? This could go on for days. He'd better end the interview, fast.

"OK. That about does it. Look, if any of you have any more information to add, just give me a call. The adult leaders have my number."

Pug left quickly, feeling he had dodged a potential barrage of teenage complaints. He'd touch base with the Georgis kid to tidy things up and then get the hell out of there. It was time to get on with the rest of his life.

When he got back to the office, Pug flipped through his phone messages. One made him stop. It came from Kaioga City, a number he knew well. As Pug crinkled the drab green message sheet, he realized that maybe he'd gone a bit too far with his fun, especially with the adult leaders.

Pug dialed slowly. The cold, piercing voice at the other end didn't use ifs, ands, or buts. *Just get the blasted thing over with, Pug.* The voice would be damned if he wanted weeks of calls from parents wondering what happened at Matulia and worrying about their kids' safety. Close it out now! Pug assured him that everything was under control. After the call, Pug scrawled a few sentences officially closing the case and handing it to his secretary to type. Scrub Saturday morning interviews.

As Pug relaxed that night in his frayed easy chair, his mind filled up with images of the day: the lolly path; the bump on Harry Vincent's forehead; arrogant Rocky Reynolds; the flummoxed Troop 64 adult leaders; and the scared-shitless boys of the Hawk Patrol. However, the country sleuth had overlooked one thing. Distracted because he was having so much fun when asking the question about enemies, he hadn't noticed that three of the Hawks—Chucky Karlson, Duster Fertig, and Gregory Brooks—had been pinching their thumbs and index fingers almost to the point of bleeding.

# CHAPTER 19

# THE VINCENTS

Tux Harrison expected the worst after he received Rocky Reynolds' message, immediately after Saturday breakfast, to come to his office. He breathed deeply and happily when he learned that Pug Jones had closed the investigation, confirming the coroner's conclusion that Harry Vincent had died by accident.

"But it's not over yet, Tux," cautioned Reynolds. "The Vincents are coming down today to get Harry's stuff. You've got to meet with them. And have the Hawk boys there, too, especially his close friends."

Tux nodded unenthusiastically. Insurance salesmen had to deal with lots of grieving families, but not one grieving for a son who had been placed in his safekeeping.

"Then, as soon as the Vincents leave, you've got to get ready for Visitors' Sunday and then the *Tribune* reporter. He'll probably be down Monday or Tuesday."

It never stops, thought Tux. This is just one long nightmare.

"I've got to be honest with you, Tux. I'm worried as hell about what those boys might say to the reporter. There've been lots of stories about the Vincent kid. If the reporter hears any of those, shit! In fact, that's exactly what we'd smell like. And while I'm at it, how are Marshall and Perryman holding up? Can you count on them to do the right thing?"

Tux nodded again, but without confidence. He figured he might be able to keep the kids in line, but Perryman was a loose cannon and Marshall had become unpredictable. First, however, he had to face the Vincents.

Ruth and Phil Vincent were small, simple people. Although neither was particularly outgoing, Ruth exuded a restrained warmth that made the Vincent home a regular gathering place for the Musketeers. The couple had come down the previous two years on Visitors' Sunday, which they would have done again this year, except now they couldn't. They had to come down on Saturday to avoid wall-to-wall condolences from so many other parents. That would have been too much to handle.

Tux Harrison met them at the director's lodge just after lunch. When they reached the Troop 64 compound, Ruth spied the other three Musketeers waiting for her on the top step of the Hawk tent entrance. As they approached her, she burst into tears. So did they.

Ruth Vincent had never hugged the three boys. That wasn't a Kaioga City custom. Today she did. She wrapped her short, skinny arms around them, one at a time, their tears flooding her narrow shoulders. Phil Vincent looked on, unsure of what to do. When Greg Brooks approached him, he shook the boy's hand and awkwardly placed his left hand on Greg's shoulder.

Then the Vincents, the three boys, and Tux—wary of leaving the Vincents alone, Tux stayed the entire time—sat in the warm tent for at least two hours. Ruth found herself consoling the boys, who couldn't stop sobbing. She almost couldn't find time for her own sadness. The Musketeers had been a big part of her life, Harry's life, her only child's life. Seeing how much they missed Harry gave her solace, at least for the moment.

Then came the inevitable questions about what they—meaning Harry—had done that summer at camp and what Harry had been doing the last time they saw him. She even wanted to know what he'd eaten that night and what final things he'd said. But as she began asking these final-night questions, the mood changed.

The boys talked less. They hesitated. Their answers became shorter, less descriptive. They glanced at each other constantly, as if getting approval for what they had just said.

Ruth could feel the change in the tent. It became even more awkward when she asked about the other two boys in the patrol, the greenhorns. Where were they? Chucky took the lead, explaining that Benny and Freddy were young and were having an even harder time dealing with the situation, so he had suggested that they try to keep busy with their regular activities. He hated having to lie like that, but he had to. The Musketeers had agreed that Foreskin Freddy and Flipper Green shouldn't be there. You couldn't count on them to say the right things, and they didn't know anything about the Musketeers' Vow.

When Ruth asked if she could meet the other adult leaders to thank them for all they had done for Harry, Tux continued the masquerade, duly reporting that they were out on camp assignments. He'd be damned if he would let that slippery-tongued bastard Perryman anywhere near the Vincents.

The increasingly awkward conversation dragged on until mid-afternoon, when the Vincents finally offered that they needed to get going so they could reach Kaioga City before dark. The boys seconded the importance of that early departure. All agreed silently that the time had arrived to get this over with.

The boys had packed Harry's stuff as neatly as possible, first making certain to get rid of any awkward evidence, like cigarettes or pieces of rope or notes Harry might have jotted down. They insisted on carrying the stuff to the Vincents' car.

Nobody said much as they took the long hike. The Vincents' honest invitation to the boys to come by and visit when they got home was met by the boys' mechanical promise to do so. Everybody breathed easier when the Vincents' car pulled out of the camp parking lot.

As usual, Phil Vincent did the driving. Ruth said very little but thought plenty as she replayed the afternoon. She knew something was wrong, terribly wrong. She had no idea what, but she could tell.

# CHAPTER 20

# VISITORS' SUNDAY

Visitors' Sunday turned into a nightmare. Normally one of the highlights of the two weeks, it usually teemed with parents and siblings strolling around the rolling hills and boys excitedly describing the wonders of being at Camp Matulia. But Visitors' Sunday of 1948 unfolded more like a funeral. In fact, it was, sort of.

Sundays always began the same way, breakfast followed by religious services. Protestants met in the mess hall, Catholics assembled at the main council ring, and Jews gathered at The Overlook above the winding Green River far below. This year all three services devoted time to remembering Harry Vincent, who received a silent prayer from his friends, including those who had never met him.

When parents began arriving in the late morning, the dam of emotions broke. Just about all of the parents seemed to know about Harry's death, since most of them subscribed to both the *Kaioga City Tribune* and the *Gazette*, the morning and afternoon editions of the paper. A brief but prominent notice of his death had appeared in the Friday afternoon *Gazette*, followed by an obituary in the Saturday morning *Tribune*. When parents besieged adult leaders with questions about details of Vincent's death and concerns about camp safety, leaders assured them that this was an unfortunate but rare accident. Safety ranked at the top of Matulia's list of concerns.

Prodded by parental inquiries, many boys broke down and sobbed, some pleading to be taken home, pleas almost universally rejected by parents who insisted that they tough it out. Even more scouts wished they could leave but wouldn't say anything because they didn't want to lose face in the eyes of their peers and supervisors.

The Hawks stood tall and together, the three remaining Musketeers teaming up to keep the tent in line. No more hazing of Freddy and Benny. Chucky Karlson put his arm around the two greenhorns and told them how proud he was of how they were holding up. Serious Greg Brooks assured them individually that they could count on him, that he was there to help if they had any problems. Even big, scary, moody Duster Fertig gave them a thumbs up for how well they had done. They universally assured their parents that they were doing fine and urged them not to worry.

Even a calculator couldn't have kept track of how many times Camp Director Rocky Reynolds glanced at his watch, hoping the damn thing would speed up and reach 4 p.m., when parents would start leaving and he could survey the damage. The late afternoon starting of engines provided the day's most beautiful sound, as cars began to crawl out of the camp parking lot.

At dinner that night, Rocky announced that he would like all adult leaders to remain after the meal. As he called on one troop leader after another, his assistant tallied up the number of defectors who had gone home with their parents. With relief, he looked down at the scratchings to find that he had lost only four boys, including two from Troop 64 but none from the worrisome Hawk Patrol. When he dismissed the rest of the leaders, he asked Tux and his team to stay.

"Good job, fellows. We've made it this far, so let's keep sticking together. Let me know right away if there are any problems. I haven't heard anything more about the reporter from the *Tribune.* I imagine he'll be down tomorrow or Tuesday. The Boss wants a nice feature story about the camp and the Vincent kid. The reporter will probably want to talk to the three of you and the Hawks, maybe even a few others. I don't know. We'll have to see."

Rocky looked from face to face, getting no response. He didn't feel like going on, but he knew he had to.

"Look, I've heard a couple of stories about Vincent. I'm not saying they're true. I'm just saying I've heard them. If that damn reporter hears about them, there's no telling what he'll write. The Boss is working the Kaioga City end, but it's up to you to make sure those boys are ready for the interviews. They're your kids. They're your responsibility." Reynolds' ensuing silence punctuated the threat.

The three Troop 64 leaders looked at him blankly. Each sentence out of Rocky's mouth raised the ante, drawing them more deeply into the unknown and unforeseeable. What did he want them to do? What about The Boss? They were almost afraid to ask for specifics. In fact, they were afraid to ask anything.

"We're all on the same page, right? We need to be a team and pull in the same direction. It's all about the Scouts. Our reputation is at stake. This isn't the time for—you know—for spreading rumors."

Reynolds looked from face to face: stoic Tux Harrison; flummoxed Ed Marshall; and seething Bill Perryman. How did he end up with such a collection of jerks?

"Same page? Same page, Tux? Ed? Bill?"

Harrison shook his head affirmatively. Marshall nodded robotically. Perryman's head appeared to move, barely, but at least enough for Rocky to jump on it.

"Great! Let's pull together, leaders. It's the Boy Scout way!"

Rocky strode out of the mess hall. Tux motioned toward the

trail to The Overlook. "We've got to talk, fellows. The Lordly Lions can handle the troop campfire tonight."

The three men headed silently down the trail, trying to figure out how in hell they ended up in this mess and what they needed to do to get through it.

# CHAPTER 21

• • • • • • • • •

# DECISION TIME

At The Overlook, Tux Harrison offered cigarettes to Marshall and Perryman. As they stared down into the chasm at the ghostly Green River and puffed silently—the insurance-salesman-turned-scoutmaster, the engineer-turned-counselor, and the baker-turned-Indian-lore-guru—they contemplated their options, all of them bad. Soon they began sharing them, discussing them, and arguing about them, sometimes screaming at each other.

Option One: stonewall. Say nothing to the Hawks and stop talking to each other about the situation. Refuse to talk to the reporter. Just send him to Rocky Reynolds and let that loud-mouth say whatever he wants. Option One: dead on arrival.

Option Two: blab. Tell the truth, the whole truth, and nothing but the truth. The Boy Scout way. Whatever the reporter asks, just tell him the truth. Perryman, especially, seemed eager to tell the reporter—in fact, tell everyone—what a flaming asshole Vincent really was. Tux stood his ground. No way in hell! That would be a disaster, for the camp, for the Scouts, especially for the three of them, now firmly planted in Reynolds' watch and The Boss' crosshairs.

Option Three: conspire. Agree among the three of them what they could say and not say. Tux made it clear that they needed to present a united front. Nothing controversial. Nothing negative.

"Are you saying I'm supposed to lie about that little prick Vincent?" snorted Perryman. "Say he was our best Indian dancer and that everyone wanted to be his pool buddy so they could get their nuts grabbed? Oh, I almost forgot. How much everybody loved getting their butts splashed by Vincent's lolly trap?"

Tux inspected the ground. He loved supervising boys, but trying to mediate among adults wasn't his strong point. He looked up at Perryman.

"Settle down, Bill. I know this isn't going to be easy. But it isn't about us. It's about the Scouts."

"Tux, what the hell have we been teaching the boys? To always tell the truth, right? Are you saying that's a bunch of crap?"

"Bill, I'm just saying this is not the time or the place to spread stories."

"Tux, I want a straight answer. Are you ordering me to lie to the reporter?"

"Bill, I'm telling you not to say anything that would make the Scouts look bad. That's what Rocky wants. That's what The Boss wants. That's what we *have* to do."

Option Four: manipulate. Have Tux talk to the Hawks. Ed Marshall leaned that way, but Tux firmly vetoed that option. He was not about to take total responsibility for everything that was said to the boys and, of course, any collateral damage that might ensue. He'd be damned if he would become the official fall guy for the entire camp.

Option Five: separate. The three of them should talk to the Hawks, one at a time. All three saw value in that approach. Maybe they could get the boys to open up more honestly one on one. Ultimately, however, they rejected that option. All five of the Hawks needed to hear the same message from them at the same time about their responsibilities.

Option Six: unite and command. Present a united front to the boys. Tell them exactly what to do, what they should say to the reporter, what not to say, and let it go at that. That might work. Get it over with, short and sweet. Harrison and Marshall were almost ready to agree on that one, but Perryman wouldn't let go.

"Look, you guys," growled Perryman. "That isn't enough. We've got to find out what the hell's been going on in the Hawk tent, everything about Vincent. If we don't find out and things explode, then it's our asses, all of our asses. Just think about some Hawk story in the *Tribune* and The Boss asking us why we didn't know about it and Rocky telling him that we knew what we were supposed to do, but we let everyone down. What are you going to say then?"

Tux didn't like the idea of questioning the boys, but he knew Perryman was probably right. Marshall felt like he was being sucked into a pit of southwestern Missouri quicksand and couldn't do anything about it.

"OK, Bill," whispered Tux. "We'll do it your way."

He stared out at the brilliant Missouri sky with the rapid emergence of the glittering constellations that he loved to talk about with the boys. As they sat silently, Tux formulated his sales pitch to the Hawks.

"How does this sound? First, we'll tell the boys that they're probably going to be interviewed by the *Tribune* reporter. Then we'll say that we've heard some stories about Vincent. After that, we'll ask if they're true and if they would share them with us, since we want to make sure of the facts. And finally, we'll explain how important it is that they only say good things about Vincent when they talk to the reporter. Does that sound like a good plan?"

Actually, it didn't. It sounded flabby and perilous. But neither Perryman nor Marshall could think of anything better.

"One more thing, fellows," added Tux.

"What?"

"Scout's Honor."

"Scout's Honor what?"

"Scout's Honor that this conversation is confidential. It stays with the three of us."

"OK."

"And Scout's Honor that not one of us is going to say anything negative about Harry Vincent to the reporter."

Perryman ground his teeth but, with Harrison and Marshall staring at him, he slowly lifted his three fingers to make the sanctified sign. As he lowered them, he muttered, "That's the first fucking time I've ever used Scout's Honor to pledge to lie."

• • • • • • • • •

# CHAPTER 22

# CONFESSIONS

By the time the three adult leaders returned to the compound, the Sunday night Troop 64 campfire had nearly ended. As the boys filed down the hill into their tents, Harrison assigned counselor Ed Marshall the duty of telling the Hawks to come up to the leaders' tent as soon as lights out had been called. This assignment rankled Marshall, but it also put him on notice that the spineless Harrison might be shoving more crap his way, especially since Tux obviously didn't trust Perryman. Oh, shit, thought Marshall. Why did he volunteer to go camping this particular summer?

Marshall didn't feel like talking to all of the Hawks, so he stopped Chucky Karlson near the water trough. "Chuck," he stammered without a lead-in, "Tux Harrison wants you to bring all of the Hawks up to the leaders' tent as soon as they call lights out." Without waiting for an answer, Marshall turned his back and walked away. He smiled knowing that he had laid the responsibility entirely on Harrison.

Chucky took slightly more care in explaining the situation to the Hawks. "Guys, I need you to be quiet and pay close attention. Don't take your shoes off. We've got to go back out in a few minutes. Tux wants the five of us to go up to the leaders' tent after they call lights out. So if you've got to take a piss, do it now. We all have to go together."

"What does Tux want?"

"Marshall didn't say. He just told me they wanted to see us."

"You all know what the hell this is about," interjected Greg Brooks. "You know what everything's about these days."

Duster Fertig lifted his huge body and walked slowly to the center of the tent. "OK, guys, this is it. This is the time for all of us to stand tall and be real Hawks. All together, right? Remember Scout's Honor. The other night—you know, on the Parade Grounds—you all pledged Scout's Honor." Duster's voice rang heavy and ominous.

He stood in front of Benny Green's bunk. Staring down, he muttered "Right, Benny."

"Right, Duster" could almost be heard.

Then he strode across to Foreskin Freddy Collins' bunk. "Right, Freddy."

"Yes, Duster."

Duster didn't bother looking at the other two Musketeers before he clambered down the stairs and headed to the lolly. All of the others followed. They had no idea how long they'd be talking to the leaders.

Chucky waited for a minute or so after lights out, then asked quietly, "Everybody ready?" He stood at the top of the tent stairs and stuck out his right hand, palm down. The other four boys stacked their right hands on top of his. "OK, let's go, Hawks."

As they reached the top of the hill, Chucky paused when he saw that the leaders had dropped the tent flaps to give them more privacy. They could only see three huge shadows illuminated by Coleman lanterns. Chucky knocked on the top step.

"Mr. Harrison, we're here. All of us."

The front tent flap opened and the boys climbed in. The three adults were seated at the back of the tent on one of the bunks, Harrison in the middle between Perryman and Marshall. Without offering them a place to sit down, Tux launched the conversation.

"Boys, you've done very well the last couple of days. You've been fine scouts. Thanks for your cooperation."

The boys nodded, barely, before Tux continued.

"So here's the situation. The *Kaioga City Tribune* will be sending a reporter down to do a story about Harry. Actually, about Harry and the camp. He's probably going to want to interview you. Maybe all of you, maybe just some of you. I'm sure he'll want to talk to you, Chucky, as patrol leader."

The boys remained silent, realizing there was more to come. Harrison knew he had to move on to Harry Vincent, but he wasn't quite sure how. Perryman saved him, sort of.

"Look, we've heard some stories about Vincent. Some pretty awful stories. We just want to know whether or not they're true."

Now even Perryman found himself at a loss for words. He looked from face to face, trying to figure out how to get started. Oh, what the hell.

"Collins, did Vincent really depants you in the pool shower?"

Harrison jerked his head in Perryman's direction, dismayed by his directness. Marshall stared at the floor. They all waited.

"Scout's Honor, Collins," Perryman's voice grew.

"Yes, sir," Freddy replied weakly. "But it wasn't that big a deal."

"Depantsing is a *very* big deal," growled Perryman. "I'm getting sick and tired of you guys always protecting each other. Collins, I figured you were better than that! Aren't you supposed to be a good Catholic?"

The conversation wasn't going the way Tux had hoped. He was about to step in and try to calm things down when Ed Marshall snapped out of his stupor.

"Benny, you asked me to move you to another tent."

Flipper Green was aghast. He had talked to Marshall in confidence. Now Marshall was embarrassing him in front of the other Hawks.

"Tell us why, Benny."

"I don't want to change tents," Flipper answered softly. "I like being a Hawk."

"But you didn't the other day," insisted Marshall. "Why the change? Did it have something to do with Vincent?"

Increasingly upset that the leaders were picking on the two greenhorns, Chucky decided to be a leader and jump in. "Please, Mr. Marshall. Leave Benny and Freddy alone. They're good guys. It's their first summer at Matulia. This has really been hard on them."

Tux was about to speak, but Perryman pounced first. "We'll get to you, Karlson. In fact, we'll get to you right now."

Perryman paused, waiting for the silence to sink in. He was reveling in making them fess up about Harry Vincent. The little prick was going to get exposed right now.

"We've heard stories about you and the lolly trap. Not very smart for a camp veteran, someone who's supposed to be a leader, even if he does come from a hick town like Merona. Was the lolly trap one of Vincent's deals, too?"

Normally careful and restrained, cerebral Greg Brooks couldn't wait any longer. He never did like Perryman, particularly when he turned into a bully, which was much of the time. And, what the hell, they couldn't very well kick Harry Vincent out of camp now, could they?

"Yeah, Harry did it," Greg said firmly, his low, measured, snarly monotone overwhelming Perryman's shouts. "He did it great. Best lolly trap ever. Got me right on the butt."

Perryman's mouth fell open. He looked at Harrison and Marshall for support but got none.

"Me, too," added Duster, enjoying Perryman's consternation. "Harry was a genius, a lolly trap genius."

"It was so good I barely felt it when I lifted the lid," chimed in Chucky, with admiration for the way his pals had turned the tables so quickly. "The stuff came right up the pipe. That's why everyone's calling me 'Shit-Face Karlson.' They're even thinking of building a monument to me…but they had to wait until after Visitors' Sunday."

By now all five of the boys were laughing, even Freddy and Benny. Tux stepped in.

"Boys, lolly traps are no laughing matter."

"But Mr. Perryman asked about it," injected Greg. "It was such a great lolly trap, we thought Harry ought to get credit for it."

"And was he ever good at short-sheeting," muttered Duster, staring directly at Perryman.

"Were you involved in that?" shouted Perryman.

"Involved in what?" Greg parried.

"You know damn well what I'm talking about, you little creeps!"

By now the boys had the adults on the run. Freddy and Benny did their part, explaining how Harry had patiently demonstrated how to short-sheet someone. Perryman sat stunned, watching the five boys transform Harry Vincent from a felon into a folk hero. Tux Harrison didn't know how to stop the carnage.

"OK, boys, enough! Back to your tent. We'll call you if we need anything more."

As they listened to the laughs fading down the hill, the three adult leaders stared in disbelief.

"Whose stupid idea was it to talk to those little shits?" muttered Perryman.

"Shut up, Bill," Tux growled. "We all agreed. And don't forget. You suggested it."

"Maybe it wasn't such a good idea, after all," came the muted voice of Ed Marshall.

"But it's done," continued Perryman. "We did it. Now we've got to live with it. Wait until he hears those stories."

"Who?" clipped Tux.

"Who? The *Tribune* reporter. Once he gets those boys going, who knows where it will end?"

Tux suddenly realized that they hadn't finished the conversation. In his haste to clear the battlefield and get the Hawks out of the tent, he had neglected to tell them the most important thing, that they were not to share any of this with the reporter.

"Ed, get the boys back here, right now," he commanded.

"Are you sure?"

"Ed, right now!"

When the boys returned, now more subdued, Tux Harrison took charge. "Look, is there anything more we ought to know? Have you told us everything, absolutely everything?"

The boys grew silent, deadly silent. They looked back and forth at each other, waiting for someone to take the lead. Chucky knew it was his duty.

"That's it. We've told you everything. Absolutely everything. Right?"

"Right!" bellowed Duster Fertig.

"Right," the others added.

"That's good," said Harrison, rising and walking over to the boys. "Now here's the most important thing. I want you to listen carefully. When the reporter gets here…Well, what I mean is…Look, there's going to be a story in the *Tribune*. If the camp comes out looking bad, if the troop looks bad…"

Tux struggled to find the words. He couldn't, but somehow Ed Marshall did.

"Boys, the stories you just told us. You can't tell those to the reporter. It would ruin the Scouts. It would ruin everyone. And it would kill Vincent's parents. Just tell them the nice stuff about Harry. Just the nice stuff, so the reporter can write a good story. Do you understand?"

The boys understood. They understood full well. Somewhere inside the boys lay future men, struggling to emerge. Maybe that responsibility had arrived too early, but the time had come.

Chucky took the lead again. "We understand. We all understand."

"I hope damn well you understand." Bill Perryman rejoined the fray. He had finally come to his senses and fully confronted the implications if the boys spoke honestly to the reporter. They had to toe the line. "This is the Boy Scouts we're talking about. None of your sniggling little toilet jokes."

"Bill, shut up!" growled Harrison. "They understand. Don't you boys?"

The boys nodded.

"OK, boys, raise your right hands." The boys complied. "Swear by Scout's Honor that you won't share these stories with anyone."

"Anyone?" asked Flipper Green. "Not just the reporter?"

"Anyone," Harrison reconfirmed.

"Not even a priest?" asked Freddy Collins.

"Anyone!" bellowed Perryman, wondering for the moment why in the hell the Scouts had let Catholics join.

With their hands raised in the sacred sign, the five boys swore to lie under Scout's Honor. After the boys lowered their hands, the eight illuminated figures silently contemplated each other with a sense of desperation about the pact they had just sealed. In the dim light cast by the Coleman lanterns, none of the adult leaders noticed that Duster Fertig's thumb and index finger had turned beet red from being pressed together long and hard.

Finally, silently, without being dismissed, the five boys turned, climbed down the stairs, and wordlessly descended the hill toward the Hawk tent. Suddenly a gyrating Tux Harrison leaped out of the leaders' tent, screaming: "Karlson! Get back up here! This very minute!"

As the other Hawks disappeared into their tent, Chucky made his way up the path. He had never before seen this Tux, seething, slobbering.

"Karlson, that was disgusting! One of the worst displays of scout leadership I've ever seen. I'm talking about YOU, Karlson. YOU! I have never been so disappointed with one of my patrol leaders. I don't know why I ever approved you as Hawk leader. Don't you realize this isn't Merona, young man? It's Kaioga City, Karlson. You've got to live up to the standards of Kaioga City."

Stunned, Chucky could barely utter a meek "I'm sorry, Mr. Harrison."

"Sorry doesn't mean a thing. Not one damn thing. You had better shape up, Karlson. Right this minute. You and the rest of the Hawks."

"Of course, Mr. Harrison," came a tad bit firmer voice.

Tux paused, afraid he was going too far. But he knew he had to make his point, clearly and firmly, about the possible consequences.

"Let me be clear, Karlson. You are never going to get your Eagle unless I recommend you. And at this point, I'm certainly not ready to write you a letter. I don't give a damn how many merit badges you earn. Do you understand?"

Harrison watched intently as Chucky's eyes moistened in the eerie Coleman light. Tux knew he had to back off a bit, but just a bit.

"It's up to you, Karlson. You've got one week to prove to me that you're worthy of being promoted. One week. That's all. Do you hear me?"

Stunned by Tux's direct threat, Chucky could only muster a choked-up "Yes, sir."

Tux turned abruptly and climbed quickly into the leaders' tent. Dreadfully alone, truly alone, Chucky stood silently in the suddenly chill Matulia air.

# CHAPTER 23

. . . . . . . . .

# MERONA BOY

Chucky sat alone on a log next to the Parade Grounds. More alone than he had been in nearly six years, since September 1942, when he started third grade at Jonathan Norwood Elementary School. A shy, awkward kid from tiny Merona in western Kansas, the son of a determined, moderately-successful tire salesman, suddenly surrounded by the arrogantly confident children of lawyers, doctors, and engineers.

Life in Kaioga City had been bittersweet from the start for Chucky and his little sister, Marlene. Sure he appreciated his folks' sacrifices, moving from Merona and scraping up enough money to buy a small home in a solidly middle class neighborhood of south Kaioga City. Sure they now went to better schools and had more exposure to culture. Marlene was even taking piano lessons. But they both had to put up with stuff that they could only share with each other, never with their folks.

Being taunted for their flat western Kansas drawls, although Marlene seemed to be able to lose hers faster. Having to smile silently when other kids talked about their weekend trips to St. Louis or Chicago to visit museums or go to Major League ball games. Hearing his classmates carry on about country clubs he had never seen and golf lessons he would never have.

Cute, outgoing little Marlene had made friends, while insecure Chucky struggled to overcome his diffidence. At first, the tough kids at nearby Randolph Road Park took turns picking on the new outsider. When he would return home with a bloody nose, his mom pleaded with his dad to do something, but all she got was a "Chucky's got to learn to tough it out." He tried, finally holding his own one Sunday afternoon with that bully Carter Richardson until the big kids stepped in and called the fight a welcome draw.

Then came the day when Duster welcomed him. Chucky wasn't sure why, but the husky brute with the menacing glower decided to take Chucky under his wing, even letting some of his tormenters know that the kid from Merona was OK. After that, things became more tolerable.

Even then, Chucky was surprised when Duster, Greg, and Harry invited him to become a Musketeer. Not a real Musketeer, mind you, but an outsider like D'Artagnan. Fine with Chucky. He belonged, even if only sort of. D'Artagnan had made a go of it. Why couldn't he?

Yet he never knew when he would run into a Merona boy moment. In the middle of a game, particularly if he screwed up a ground ball. Or during a party when he spilled some punch or pinned the tail on the donkey's ear. Or when being introduced to a parent, noticing the flip of a head or a crinkled smile or sardonic eyes that tipped him off that he hadn't been careful enough with his speech.

But Chucky worked hard at belonging. Very hard. Maybe sometimes too hard, but it was better than not belonging, so he kept on.

When Tux Harrison named him Hawk Patrol leader, Chucky took it as another sign of progress. And he had done a good job, he hoped. He had convinced the Musketeers to take in newcomers Benny Green and Freddy Collins. He had done his best to help the two outsiders fit in, even though Harry's taunting had made this difficult.

Then came Chucky's third year at Matulia. As the new Hawk Patrol leader he had real responsibilities, like making sure everyone had smoothed out their sleeping bags, put their stuff in order before breakfast, tied up the tent flaps correctly, and did their part in cleaning the paths around the tent in preparation for the adult leaders' three-times-a-day inspection. He hadn't been doing all that well, particularly since Harry had not made any effort to help, while Freddy and Flipper, trying to win Harry's approval, began imitating Harry's nonchalance.

The tent even caught the attention of Putz Perryman, who carried out the mid-morning inspections. Sidling up to Chucky, Perryman whispered in his ear, "The Hawk Patrol tent looked like crap this morning. Get your ass in gear, Karlson. Keep this up and there'll be a new Hawk Patrol leader before camp is over."

Then came Thursday and the lolly path and the body and the sheriff and the Vincents. Chucky had tried so hard during those last few days. But for what? He was falling behind in his merit badge classes, badges he had to earn for his Eagle. Now, out of nowhere, Tux Harrison was making it all seem worthless.

How could Chucky explain this to his folks? After what they had done for him, knowing how proud they were of his becoming a patrol leader, knowing what hopes they had placed in him. He clenched his left fist and pounded it into the dirt. Chucky was on his own. But he had made it this far. He wasn't going to quit now.

When Chucky got back to the tent, the rest of the boys were asleep. Or at least they played as if they were. Chucky lay down, dead tired, but too wound up to sleep. Fuck Tux Harrison. Fuck Harry Vincent. Fuck Kaioga City. Fuck them all. Tomorrow would be Chucky Karlson time.

# PART III

# UNFINISHED STORY

# CHAPTER 24

# LETTER TO RUTH VINCENT

*Dear Ruth,*

*Please accept my apologies for having been so delinquent in writing you. I have been very busy. However, I realize that this is not an acceptable reason for my negligence. Everybody is busy.*

*I hope that things have been better for you since the last time we wrote. Has your arthritis improved? Were you able to take that trip to Denver that you had been planning?*

*I have a piece of news I hope will please you. I have just signed a contract to write a new book. At this point it is called "Unfinished Stories." It will be about some of my past stories, stories that were published prematurely, before I could explore everything that I would have liked to do. That's the way it is in the daily newspaper business. Deadlines, deadlines, deadlines. I'm not making excuses. That's just the nature of our profession.*

*This new book gives me the opportunity to do something I have always wanted to do—actually complete those stories. The most important story is the one I wrote for the Kaioga City Tribune thirty-six years ago, back in 1948, the one about your wonderful little boy, Harry.*

*I did the best I could at the time, but my editor was so anxious to run the story that he wouldn't give me time to do any more research. As you know, it won several journalism prizes, but it could have been better. Now it will be.*

*Harry's story will be the first one in the book. The complete story. The story I could have written in 1948 if I had had more time. I plan to interview as many of Harry's friends as I can find. Most of all, I would love to talk to you again.*

*I realize that we haven't seen each other since the Eagle Scout ceremony in 1948, but I have cherished our correspondence and I very much treasure our long-distance friendship. If it is not too much of an intrusion on your life, I would like to spend some time with you when I am in Kaioga City doing my research.*

*Thank you again for your friendship and your willingness to consider my request.*

*Sincerely,*

*Ardith (Millett) Cunningham*

\* \* \*

As she had so many times before in the last few weeks, Ardith hesitated, indecisive, pondering whether or not to send the letter—the solemn promise—to Ruth Vincent. But this time she didn't crumple it up or rip it into shreds. Instead she decided to let it rest on her desk until the next morning. Then she could make her choice. discard it or send it, sealing her pledge to Ruth, her pledge to discover and write Harry's full story.

Ardith wasn't certain she was ready for that journey, but she knew she couldn't avoid it forever. The story of Harry Vincent had to be told. It should be told while her aging friend was still alive, to provide closure for that aching woman.

Then she eyed the paperweight, the national journalism award she had won for her 1948 story about Harry. The lie that had made her career. For more than three decades Ardith had kept the paperweight on her desk as a reminder, the reminder of a story unfinished, of an obligation unfulfilled. It was a weight she could no longer bear.

Ardith half smiled. Slowly nodding, she folded the letter and slid it into the envelope addressed to Kaioga City. She didn't have to wait until tomorrow. She would mail it that evening.

• • • • • • • • •

# CHAPTER 25

# HUMAN INTEREST

I know a veteran journalist shouldn't begin a story by saying I'm sorry. But I have to. I am sorry, terribly sorry, about the first big story I ever wrote. It happened in 1948 while I was a young reporter, not long after I had graduated from the University of Missouri.

\* \* \*

"Ardie, I've got a nice little human-interest story for you."

Ardith Millett could hear those words even before *Tribune* City Editor Roger Hackford opened his mouth. She was almost right.

"Ardie, remember that story we ran about the kid who died at Camp Matulia last week? You know, that Boy Scout? Harry Vincent was his name. Why don't you go down to Matulia, check it out, and write me a nice little human-interest story about the kid? And while you're at it, Ardie, include something about the camp itself. Make it for a Sunday feature."

Whenever Hackford waved her over to his desk, Ardith knew it would be a nice little human-interest story. Never a contentious city council meeting or a juicy murder or other front-page stuff, like a good corruption scandal. Always a human-interest story. It was the same for the other two female reporters at the *Kaioga City Tribune*. Always human-interest stories, as if that's what women were biologically predisposed to write.

"Yeah, take a run down to Camp Matulia and see what you can find out about the Vincent kid."

"Thank you, Mr. Hackford. Is it OK if I go down tomorrow? Do some background reading today?"

"Sure. That's fine. If you can get it to me by Friday afternoon, we'll see if we can squeeze it into next Sunday's 'Around K. C.' section. If not, the week after. No big rush, Ardie."

There was never any big rush on most of her stories. They weren't that important. She'd heard "No big rush, Ardie" enough times. In fact, she'd heard "Ardie" more than enough times.

Ardith couldn't understand why Hackford kept calling her "Ardie". She'd never been called that before, not growing up in Waverly, not in college. But for some reason Hackford stuck it on her the day she arrived. She didn't like it but, by the time she decided she ought to say something, he had used it so often that it would have been awkward to correct him, so she clammed up and accepted it. However, she did make certain that her article bylines read Ardith, not Ardie, Millett.

Ardith smiled sweetly. "That will be nice, thank you. I've never been to Southwest Missouri."

"Oh, in that case, why don't you spend the night down there," Hackford said, making the invitation sound like an order. "Drive down tomorrow morning. Spend the afternoon at the camp. We'll cover a night at the Hexterville Hotel. Be sure to set up a talk with Harry's family when you get back. Make a real story out of it."

Sure, make a real story out of it. Ardith knew that, in Hackford's mind, it wasn't a "real" story, but maybe she could do something with it. At least while she was down at Matulia she couldn't be asked to cover a Red Cross benefit or the opening of some shopping corner.

"Thank you, Mr. Hackford. I'll do that."

Three "thank you's" in one conversation, thought Ardith. She'd never heard the other reporters—make that, the male reporters—thank Hackford that many times when they got their assignments. She was trying to break the habit, but it came so naturally to her. One "thank you" would have been just fine, but the others kept popping out of her mouth.

"Oh, one more thing, Ardie. Go easy on the Vincents. It's been a rough week for them. You know, sending their boy down to camp and him coming back dead. So be careful."

"Thank you for the advice, Mr. Hackford," Ardith answered, kicking herself for "thank you" number four. She swore she would break that habit when she got back.

Ardith read through the obituary and the news item about Harry's death. Not much there. Harry Vincent had fallen, hit the back of his head, and died. The first time a scout had died at Camp Matulia. Maybe that would be the peg to hang the story on.

Ruth Vincent's faint voice on the phone didn't provide much more promise. Yes, she would be glad to talk to Ardith on Thursday morning at her home, a Randolph Road address near Jonathan Norwood Elementary School. Those thirty telephone seconds made clear to Ardith that she didn't look forward to talking to Ruth Vincent. This would be her first interview with a grieving mother. She began to regret her many "thank you's," but there was no turning back.

*OK, Ardith. You're a journalist.* She looked over at Elmont Taylor, one of the *Tribune's* hotshot young reporters. He wouldn't give a second thought about interviewing the Vincents. He'd barge right in, ask tough questions, open some wounds, and get a good story, maybe even some blood-soaked quotes. *You're up to it, Ardith. But do it your way. Think of this as an opportunity, not just an assignment.*

Ardith went to the *Tribune* archives and found several articles about Camp Matulia. Colorful, but nothing very exciting. Young boys having fun and learning all sorts of outdoor things. Boys on the road to becoming men. Boys being trained to become future leaders of Kaioga City. She could have written those stories.

But none of them had much to do with her challenge. Ardith fell asleep that night thinking about death and woke up at 4 a.m. worrying about Ruth Vincent.

. . . . . . . . .

# CHAPTER 26

# SMALL TOWN GIRL

Above all, journalists should have courage and honesty. Unfortunately, I began my career by being a coward and a liar. It happened during my first full-time professional job, at the Kaioga City Tribune.

* * *

Ardith Millett soon realized how much she detested the hot morning drive down to Camp Matulia. While she enjoyed looking at the spooky forests and rolling hills of Southwest Missouri, she became angrier and angrier over where the road was taking her. She had left Waverly in North Central Missouri to get away from home. Now she was heading back.

So what if they called it Hexterville instead of Waverly. It was the small-town life she had tried to escape. A life without privacy. A life where everybody knew too much about you and talked about you even if they didn't know. A life as an outsider because she was shy, got good grades, didn't have any boobs, and had never gone steady because she wouldn't put out, at least put out the way that Waverly guys expected. A life without a future for a woman who dreamed of being something special, not just get married, have kids, and talk to the other girls who stayed home.

Of course she wanted to get married and have kids, but she also wanted something else, although she wasn't quite sure what. That's why she chose the University of Missouri. Sure,

Columbia was a small town, too, but Mizzou was lively and had a wonderful journalism school. She even began to like dating, because some Mizzou guys didn't expect you to put out, that is, *really* put out, so she could relax more and enjoy letting her special friends hold her tiny boobs, sometimes her bare boobs.

Ardith didn't exactly like the way guys talked, especially about girls. Even after a nice evening out, she would go back to the small upstairs bedroom she rented from the Williams family and think about the guys' conversations when they got back to the frat house.

"What did you get with Millett?"

"I got bare boobs."

"Bare boobs? Great? Did you get bare pussy?"

She imagined the lies they might have told to answer that last question but knew she couldn't do anything about it. She didn't want to spend every night alone in the Williams' bedroom, so she'd have to put up with skuzzy frat talk about what they "got" from her. It would be better when she started a job with one of the St. Louis or Chicago newspapers.

Except she didn't end up in St. Louis or Chicago. She applied, but they turned her down, just like most of the other girls in the J-School. They didn't need any more women. They already had a few. She did receive a couple of offers from small town papers, but this was exactly what she was trying to get away from. So she considered it the happiest moment of her life when the *Kaioga City Tribune* wrote and asked her to join the staff. Kaioga City wasn't St. Louis or Chicago, but it had beautiful hills, lots of nice fountains, good hamburgers, a minor league baseball team, a symphony orchestra, and opportunity.

At least she thought it had opportunity. But then came the "women's assignments" to cover social events. Stories about high school graduations and profiles of girls, always girls, like those who had been elected homecoming queen, which had never happened to her. So here it was, two years later, two years of stories about fashion shows, Presbyterian weddings, and restaurant re-openings. Now she was getting ready to write about a dead boy nobody cared about while sweating because the eastern sun poured into her window as she drove south to another of those damn small towns she thought she had escaped. She opened all of the windows, but it didn't help much because the rain that had blown through an hour earlier had left the air oppressively muggy, as it had been just about every day the past week.

Downtown Hexterville wasn't worse than she expected, but it was bad enough. A pool hall, a jewelry shop with a bald-headed man repairing watches in the front window, a crummy five-and-dime store, and an even crummier hotel with a still crummier room. At least there was a movie house with a film she had already seen and a soda fountain where she could go after she got back from Camp Matulia.

Leaving her bruised suitcase in the hotel room, Ardith sidled into a booth at the frayed diner down the street. Nothing on the soiled menu looked particularly interesting, so she chose the corn beef hash special with French fries and coleslaw scrawled on the chipped blackboard. As she poked her way through the heaped meal, she realized she wasn't all that hungry. She had too many concerns: What was she going to ask these scouts about their dear dead friend? She still hadn't completely decided what to ask when she climbed into her car and headed off for Camp Matulia, a twisty, dusty seven miles away.

· · · · · · · · ·

# CHAPTER 27

# BOY TALK

Women have never had it easy in the newspaper world. Maybe that helps to explain—not excuse—something I did at the beginning of my career.

\* \* \*

Ardith didn't expect trumpets and elephants to greet her at Camp Matulia, and she was right. A tall, skinny local wearing a straw hat opened the sagging gate and motioned her to the muddy parking lot. A melting sign pointed to the administration lodge, where a woman at a sagging wooden desk greeted her and told her the camp director would be back soon.

Rocky Reynolds strode in shortly after lunch, walking right past her. "When the *Tribune* reporter gets here, send him in," he told his secretary without pausing as he closed his office door. The secretary waited a couple of minutes, then told Ardith she could go in. Opening his door after hearing her polite knock, Reynolds stared incredulously.

"Hello, I'm Ardith Millett from the *Kaioga City Tribune*."

It took Reynolds a few moments to grasp the fact that this actually was the reporter, not a reporter's assistant. Then he smiled and pointed to a chair, followed by "Have a seat, honey."

Ardith didn't need her questions, because Rocky never stopped talking. The beauty of the camp. How much fun the boys were having. What they were learning. What they did every day, from having three hearty meals to taking merit badge classes to swimming to playing softball games after dinner to enjoying evening campfires. What a wonderful safety record they had and how Harry Vincent's death was such an aberration. Ardith jotted down some notes, even though she didn't need to since she had read most of this stuff in the *Tribune* archive.

Without having paused for questions, Reynolds dismissively concluded the interview with "I suppose you might want to talk to someone in Harry's troop. I'll walk you over." Rocky figured he'd better make sure she got right to Tux Harrison, who knew what he was supposed to do. He sure didn't want her stumbling across big-mouth Bill Perryman alone.

As Rocky babbled on, Ardith became aware of how inappropriately she had dressed. Roger Hackford insisted that women wear hosiery and high heels into the newsroom and on assignments, but Ardith's ankles were already rebelling as her angular shoes did battle with Matulia's rocks, gravel, and uneven terrain.

Tux Harrison was waiting awkwardly in front of the leaders' tent. He had planned to invite the reporter to sit on one of the beds but hadn't expected this reporter. Too late to change plans now, he motioned to the stairs.

Sitting across from Ardith, Tux softly described the beauty of their compound and led her through the troop's daily activities, a more low-key version of Rocky Reynolds' soliloquy. Unlike Reynolds, however, he ended his monologue by asking her if she had any more questions. In fact, she hadn't asked any.

"Yes, Mr. Harrison, could you tell me a bit about Harry Vincent and the day he died?"

Tux answered courteously, providing little that Ardith hadn't already read in the news story and obituary. As the interview proceeded, Harrison's "yeses" and "no's" came to dominate, with minimal elaboration.

Yes, Harry Vincent was a nice boy. Yes, he was very popular in the troop. No, there was nothing special about him, just a fine young man striving to become an Eagle Scout. Yes, what happened was so sad. Yes, he was the first camper who had ever died at Camp Matulia. No, nobody had seen him die. Yes, they had reported it to the sheriff, just as they were supposed to do. Yes, his body had been sent back to Kaioga City for burial. Yes, his parents had come down on Saturday to pick up his stuff. No, as the scoutmaster he was trying to maintain the regular routine because he owed it to the rest of the boys. Yes, the boys were doing fine under the circumstances.

"Maybe you ought to meet my two assistants," interjected Harrison. He called Perryman and Marshall, who had been hanging around waiting for their tour of duty. But their answers didn't add much to what Harrison and Reynolds had already said. Marshall did most of the talking, with Perryman saying little, particularly when it came to her questions about Vincent.

"Are you interested in spending a few minutes with the Hawk Patrol?" asked Tux. "That's the one Harry belonged to." Of course Ardith was interested. She needed a story. She desperately needed a story. "They're at their afternoon merit badge classes right now, but they should be back pretty soon."

In the meantime, Ardith was welcome to walk around the compound. There weren't any outhouses for women, but she could use the mess hall bathroom for the women who worked in the kitchen. Ardith didn't want to brave the long, rocky walk to and from the mess hall, so she asked to see the place where Harry's body was found. Tux offered one of the Lordly Lions, Eddie Simpson, whom Tux had asked to stick around for such a possibility.

Eddie led Ardith down the lolly path. As she slipped and slid, Ardith again cursed her lack of common sense in choosing the day's footwear. Of course Harry Vincent could have fallen on this steep path. Lots of other kids must have fallen and hurt themselves, too.

As she worked her way down the path her "what in the hell is that" sense of smell awoke. The stench was overwhelming. Eddie snickered at her lack of awareness.

"Oh, that's just the lolly."

"The what?"

"The lolly. There. The six-holer," he said, motioning to the shed.

"Is that what you all use?"

"Sure, if we have to." He grinned. "If we can't avoid it."

As she stared down at the ramshackle brown structure, Ardith pondered the possibility of

a story about sixty-five scouts sharing a stinking six-hole outhouse for two weeks. Now that would be a real human-interest story. On second thought, she couldn't imagine Roger Hackford running a story, "Soaring Smells from a Scout Six-Holer," no matter how beautifully alliterative the headline, even if she changed "Soaring" to "Soothing" or even "Sensuous."

Ignoring—or trying to ignore—the smell wafting up from the latrine, Ardith sketched the lolly path, marking the place where Harry had fallen. As she stood at the sharp zig of the path where Terry Fleener had found Vincent's body, she noted how secluded it was, barely visible through the trees from either the compound or the lolly. Inspecting the rugged, twisting, tree-filled terrain, Ardith could understand how Harry might well have fallen without anyone seeing him.

After the unrevealing interviews with Reynolds and the Troop 64 leaders, Ardith was anxious to talk to the Hawks.

She grew even more anxious after she talked to them, since the five Hawks weren't any more forthcoming than the adult leaders. Swell guy. Nice friend. Good scout. Nothing special. They would miss him. They were doing fine. Ardith's pencil rested idly in her lap. "Nice friend" and "swell guy" weren't going to get her story on the front page of the Around Kaioga City section. "Fine young man" and "a credit to the Boy Scouts" wouldn't convince Roger Hackford to give her a rousing "Attagirl."

Tux Harrison, who had taken her to the Hawk tent, had told her to wait, that he would be by to get her after her interview so he could escort her back to the director's lodge. But recognizing she wasn't getting anywhere, Ardith cut short the Hawk interview, thanked the boys, and began to wander around the compound. Ardith's pad didn't contain many interesting notes.

That is, she didn't have many notes until she passed the water trough and ran into Eldon Reeble, a red-haired, freckle-faced boy who belonged to the Frog Patrol and seemed delighted to talk about Harry Vincent. Harry was special. He was funny, really funny. He liked to tell jokes. He liked to play pranks. He made everybody laugh.

She soon heard similar things from other scouts who gathered around this strange girl all dressed up in heels and a dust-covered dress. They seemed to know Harry so much better than the Hawks did. Harry was lively. He was neat to be around. He said crazy things. He did crazy things, like...

The word "crazy" pierced Ardith, over and over, as she listened to the boys' abundant Harry Vincent lore. Crazy things. Maybe there was a story here, a real story, not just a woman's story. Now she had questions, good questions, for the Hawks. As she headed back toward their tent, Ardith was thinking about the story and what she was going to ask the Hawks. She was thinking so much that she forgot she was wearing heels.

When her feet flew out from under her, she flopped on her back, her head barely missing a jagged rock.

Staring up at the concerned young faces encircling her, Ardith began forming a story in her head. Just began, no more. But at least she had begun. There was more digging to do.

Tux Harrison's ashen face joined the boys. "Are you OK, Miss Millett?" As they helped her up, Tux added, "I told you to stay at the Hawk tent."

"Told" met "crazy" in Ardith's head. The scoutmaster seemed more concerned that she had gone out wandering on her own than that she had fallen down. She voiced a silent thanks to Eldon Reeble and his friends.

By now it was late in the afternoon. Ardith changed her mind about continuing with the Hawks. They probably weren't going to tell her much more than she hadn't already gotten from Eldon Reeble and the other scouts at the water trough. She needed to escape from Tux Harrison's hovering and Rocky Reynolds' relentless pitch. For the moment, she merely admired the ruggedly beautiful and surprisingly charming camp. *The kind of place I'd like to send my boys*, Ardith thought, *that is, if I ever have boys. If I have kids. If I get married.* If she were doing anything but trying to penetrate this curtain of words that, until the last few minutes, seemed to be dedicated to preventing her from discovering something to write about, something that was both human and interesting.

The camp leaders were courteous, even inviting her to stay for dinner. At first, she considered accepting, thinking she might stumble onto something else, but she quickly admitted to herself that this would just mean another hour of smoke-screens. She needed time to think. Thanking Reynolds and Harrison for their courtesy, she headed back into Hexterville.

*Double Indemnity* was playing at the downtown movie house. Ardith had seen that murder story before, actually a couple of times, back in college. *I guess that's how long it took for stuff to get to Hexterville.* Because she knew the intricate plot well enough, she only half watched the movie. Instead she tried to unravel her own mystery.

• • • • • • • • •

# CHAPTER 28

# ROCKY REYNOLDS

Camp Director Rocky Reynolds took a deep breath as he watched Ardith Millett drive down the road toward Hexterville. Why in the hell did the *Tribune* send a mousy, flat-chested girl to do a story about Matulia? Wasn't the camp important enough to send a real reporter?

Or maybe those Kaioga City folks were smarter than he gave them credit for. What if the paper did this on purpose, knowing she wouldn't be up to asking tough questions? Maybe The Boss had something to do with it. The Boss. Always the fucking Boss. Always at least one step ahead of everyone else.

The Boss could do everything. That included making certain that Rocky never got the credit he deserved for running Matulia. Every time some eastern scout leaders came to look at the camp, The Boss showed up to receive the accolades.

Well, the little prick did know how to get things done. He had managed to get the *Tribune* to send a sappy girl instead of some inquisitive guy. Rocky had to smile as he thought of The Boss' cleverness at pulling that one off.

But Rocky knew he wasn't fully out of the woods. The session still had three more full days before the boys headed back to Kaioga City. He had to make damn sure there were no more explosions, especially involving Troop 64. Rocky pondered his dilemma.

Tux Harrison looked as if he was about to come apart. Anyway, Rocky had never fully relied on Harrison. Too stiff, too soft, too formal, too indecisive. Harrison could be OK when things were running smoothly, but not when there was trouble.

Bill Perryman was worse. Good Indian dancer, knew his stuff about Indian lore, but what an asshole. He could have blown the entire thing. He could still blow it. Got to keep that guy in check.

This left Ed Marshall. Who in the hell is Ed Marshall? First year at camp. Not much personality. Hasn't shown him shit. What an option! But Rocky had no choice. He had to lean on Marshall. Rocky sent a runner down to the 64 compound. A half hour later he came back with Marshall.

"Hi, Ed. Have a seat!"

Marshall offered a soft hello, then sat down quietly, waiting for Rocky to take the lead. Rocky looked at the squat, flabby engineer. Is it worth the risk? What other options do I have?

"Ed, I need your help."

"Yes, Rocky."

"I've been watching Troop 64, and I think it needs new leadership."

"New leadership?"

"Yeah. I mean, I'm not going to replace Tux Harrison. He's been around a long time. Done a pretty good job. Knows how to keep things rolling. But we've got a special situation right now. Somebody's got to keep an eye on things in 64, especially the Hawks, and be ready to make tough decisions. You're the man."

"What about Bill Perryman? He's got more experience."

Rocky stared at Marshall. Should he tell him he didn't trust that temperamental son of a bitch? No, he didn't know Marshall well enough.

"Perryman's fine, but he's better sticking to his Indian thing.

He wouldn't have time to do what I need."

"What would you like me to do, Rocky?"

"Make decisions, man. Make tough decisions. If you see something going on, make decisions and tell me."

"Should I clear them with Tux?"

Thinking about the indecisive Harrison, Rocky walked over to Marshall and put his right hand on Ed's left knee.

"Look, Ed. I've been watching you. I think you've got real leadership qualities. No, you don't have to clear everything with Tux. Just act, tell me, and I'll stand behind you."

Marshall nodded. "I'll do my best, Rocky. I'll try not to let you down."

"You'll do great, Ed. I know you will."

As Marshall slowly walked away from the administrative cabin, Reynolds watched, hoping he'd done the right thing. He'd rolled the dice. If Marshall screwed up and Tux informed The Boss, Rocky's ass would be cooked. He'd never get a good letter of recommendation if he applied to be the leader of some other big city scout council, which is what he wanted.

But if Marshall came through and the rest of the session passed uneventfully, Rocky could take full credit for leading the camp through a serious crisis. He'd shown that he wasn't just an extension of The Boss. Rocky smiled as he thought about Marshall. Maybe that quiet little guy will be just what he needed.

. . . . . . . . .

# CHAPTER 29

# ED MARSHALL

Ed Marshall slowly walked away from the director's cabin. By the time he reached the Troop 64 compound, his stroll had turned into a strut. After nine days of being the junior partner, trapped between the cold, autocratic Harrison and the hot-headed, overbearing Perryman, Marshall relished the freedom to act, particularly with Camp Director Rocky Reynolds behind him.

His first opportunity came quickly, maybe too quickly. Spotting Chucky Karlson, Ed went up to the Hawk leader and draped his arm over the boy's shoulders.

"Chucky, you've been doing a fine job under very tough conditions. I'm really proud of you." After a brief pause, he made his gambit. "If you need anything, just come to me. Privately. I'll see what I can do."

Chucky stared at this new Ed Marshall. Maybe this was the break Chucky had been looking for to turn things around. After a moment, he decided to take advantage of the adult leader's offer.

"Thank you, Mr. Marshall. I do have a favor to ask."

"What is it?"

"I'd like to split up the Hawks."

"Split up the Hawks?"

"Yes, after what happened, it's kind of hard being together so much."

Ed Marshall wasn't ready for such drastic action.

"It would be awfully hard to rearrange tents this late in the session."

"I guess we can handle being in the same tent. We just sleep there. It's the meals. They're tough. It's so hard to talk to each other."

Marshall smiled. Here was his chance to be decisive, to act without consulting with Harrison or Perryman.

"Sure, Chucky. I understand your situation. Let me see what I can do. Thanks for confiding in me. I'm here for you whenever you want."

Marshall watched the Hawk table that night at dinner. Hardly a word was spoken. The boys seldom looked up from their plates. After dinner, Ed went from tent to tent, finally getting agreement from five patrols to let one Hawk eat at their tables for the rest of the week. That night, just before lights out, he broke the news to the Hawks. He received no objection. The next morning, Ed offhandedly mentioned his action to Tux Harrison.

"Why didn't you clear this with me first?"

Ed smiled and said, in a low but firm voice, "It needed to be done."

Tux said nothing more. Not then, not for the rest of the session when Ed repeatedly acted on his own, shredding the troop hierarchy. Marshall paid special attention to the Hawks, who no longer ate together, swam together, sat together at evening campfires, or spent much time in the tent except for sleeping. He made certain to greet each of them every day and ask if they needed anything from him, but they didn't have much to say to him, except for Chucky, who thanked Marshall for his support, especially finding them new tables.

Chucky could have blessed Marshall. With the Hawks now under control, he turned his full attention to his merit badges.

When his Bird Study counselor patted him on the back that Friday and congratulated him on his good project, Chucky knew he had cleared all but the final hurdle. Then, that last night at the general campfire, Tux Harrison smiled at him and softly offered, "Nice work, Chucky. You came through."

Ed Marshall repeatedly dropped in on Rocky Reynolds, his benefactor, to share his successes. By Friday Rocky had become bored with his increasingly pompous protégé, but he took pride in having bet on the right horse. When the boys climbed into their buses that Saturday morning to head back to Kaioga City, Rocky relaxed with the knowledge that he had weathered the storm and had demonstrated what a great crisis leader he could be. Somebody was bound to notice.

· · · · · · · · ·

# CHAPTER 30

# CORONER'S REPORT

*A fourteen-year-old Boy Scout named Harry Vincent died at a Southwest Missouri scout camp in 1948 under mysterious circumstances, and I helped cover it up. Now I'm going to try to uncover it.*

\* \* \*

On Wednesday morning, Ardith Millett woke up ready to go. Not right back to Kaioga City. It didn't make sense to rush since she wouldn't be interviewing Ruth Vincent until Thursday. She needed details. Roger Hackford was a stickler for details and she didn't want to have to drive all the way back down in case she had overlooked something.

After breakfast she headed for the county coroner's office to see if his report contained anything important that hadn't appeared in the obituary. It didn't...at least not on the first reading. But since the report wasn't very long, she perused it two more times. Not until the third reading did Ardith fix on the single sentence about the bump on Harry Vincent's forehead.

As she savored that sentence, she recalled the concerned faces of the Troop 64 boys staring down at her, sprawled on her back on that Matulia hill. She had hit the ground hard and just lay there. Harry had fallen hard, too, hard enough to cause a severe concussion to the back of his head. The back of his head, not his forehead. So how did he get a bump on his forehead? He couldn't have fallen face first, then bounced so high that he came down hard enough on his back to kill himself.

Ardith paused. Get ahold of yourself. Maybe all of those human-interest assignments had made her hungry for a juicier story. Maybe too hungry. Too many murder movies like *Double Indemnity*. Maybe she was letting her imagination get the best of her.

So what? Here she was, already in Hexterville. It wouldn't hurt to at least ask for some clarification. After all, Roger Hackford loved details.

Ardith lucked out. County Coroner Mike Maldeth happened to be in his office. No deaths today at Matulia, she mused. No kids being run over by tractors or wives shooting their ex-husbands who had been abusing them or farm kids killed in a pitchfork fight. Maldeth greeted her with a sense of bored hospitality. Sure, he'd be glad to help, if he could. But Maldeth didn't help much.

"The bump on his forehead? Oh, the bump on his forehead. Nothing important. I just like to make my reports as complete as possible. Probably hit his head on some tree limb or maybe a tent post. You know, these kids walk around in the dark. They can be pretty careless. The main thing is—he fell on his back and the back of his head hit a rock, hit it hard. Kind of a freak accident, but it's the sort of thing that happens now and then in these woods."

"But, Dr. Maldeth, isn't it possible that the bump on Vincent's forehead might have had some connection to his fall?"

"Like what?"

"I don't know. Maybe he bumped up against something and it knocked him down." Ardith paused. "Or maybe somebody hit him."

Maldeth looked at her intently, then gradually smiled, a nice paternalistic smirk. "Miss—what was your name?"

"Millett."

"Miss Millett, not Mrs. Millett?"

"Miss Millett."

"Look, Miss Millett, there's no reason to start imagining things. I took a good look at the body and the location. So did the sheriff. We both came to the same conclusion, a pretty obvious one. Harry Vincent slipped, fell, and hit the back of his head. People are always falling down in these hills. It's just not very often that someone hits his head on a rock and dies."

Ardith wasn't sure how to proceed. Neither was Maldeth, who by now was breathing deeply as he continued.

"I base my reports on facts, not on conjecture. Those are the facts. That's why I put them in my report."

Maldeth took another deep breath and waited for Ardith's next question, but not for long. Silences bothered him.

"Look, is there anything else I can do for you, sweetie?"

Ardith was about to ask more about the bump, but the "sweetie" froze her. She decided she didn't want to deal with another brush off or the degrading laugh she was sure to provoke if she continued to pursue that line of questioning.

*Control yourself, Ardith.* If she keeps this up, Maldeth might complain to the *Tribune.* She could hear him telling Hackford or some other *Tribune* editor that their "sweetie" had let her imagination run wild, that next time he ought to send one of the guys, maybe that funny dude who used to play tackle for North High.

"Thank you, Dr. Maldeth. You've been very helpful." Ardith wasn't sure why she added, "I'll be sure to verify your story with the sheriff."

Watching Ardith walk to her car, Maldeth tapped the telephone. As she drove off, he picked it up and dialed. "Hi, Pug. I want to tip you off. The *Tribune* reporter's on the way to see you. Can you believe it? They sent some gal with a wild imagination, asking crazy questions." Maldeth paused. "Pug, I may have screwed up in my report on the Vincent kid. Maybe I shouldn't have mentioned that bump on his forehead."

• • • • • • • • •

# CHAPTER 31

# RUTH VINCENT

*A devoted mother suffered, suffered greatly, when her son died under mysterious circumstances in 1948 at Boy Scout Camp Matulia in southwest Missouri. Because of my personal weaknesses, I unintentionally but inexcusably added to her suffering. I was wrong then; now I'm going to try to make it right.*

\* \* \*

The trip down south had raised the stakes for Ardith's upcoming interview with Ruth Vincent. In Ardith's mind, the human-interest story about a dead boy had been transformed into a mystery about the cause of his death. She worried that she might be letting her imagination run amok, but so many things didn't make sense to her.

Rocky Reynolds' refusal to let her ask questions. Tux Harrison's brusque answers. The unresponsiveness of the Hawks, so discordant when contrasted with the other scouts' stories about crazy Harry Vincent. The bump on Harry's forehead. Her own fall at Matulia. Mike Maldeth's adamant rejection of her perfectly reasonable alternative explanation. Finally, the unavailability of Sheriff Lester Jones, whom his secretary insisted would be gone all day.

Ardith's mind ricocheted between the belief that she was uncovering an enormous conspiracy and the fear that she had completely lost her bearings. Maybe talking to Ruth Vincent would settle things down and get her back on track. Or maybe it would bring greater clarity to the significance of the past week's events. Those thoughts were on her mind as she rang the doorbell of the modest two-story home on Randolph Road. A short, soft-spoken, seemingly unremarkable woman came to the door.

"Mrs. Vincent?"

"Yes."

"I'm Ardith Millett from the *Tribune*. Thank you so much for taking this precious time to talk to me. I'll try not to be too much of a burden."

Ruth Vincent led Ardith into their compact living room. Harry's photograph sat on a small cherry upright piano tucked into an alcove. The sheet music sat open to a simple Chopin étude.

"Do you play, Mrs. Vincent?"

Ruth slammed the keyboard cover, shaking the bland unlit yellow lamp and knocking Chopin to the floor.

"No, but Harry does. Harry did. That's Harry. He wasn't very advanced, but he loved playing."

As Ardith leaned down to pick up the fallen music, Ruth barked, "Leave them!" while motioning for Ardith to sit down. Ardith settled uncomfortably into a soft pale green chair with doilies on the arm rests. While Ruth went to get a tray of tea and cookies, Ardith looked around the room, illuminated by a single lamp set on dim. Ruth returned, then carefully poured two cups and held out the plate of cookies. Although she wasn't hungry, Ardith couldn't say no.

The conversation began the only way it could, awkwardly. Ardith stammered in repetitious detail that she was going to write a feature story about Harry and wanted to learn as much as she could so that she could do justice to the young man.

"Justice?" Ruth asked coldly. "What's justice when my little Harry is dead? Last week I sent him down to scout camp. He came home dead. How can there be any justice in that? You can't write justice!"

Ruth looked down, then continued. "I'm sorry. I shouldn't have said that. You seem like a fine young lady. I know you're trying to write a nice story. I'll try to help you."

Ruth Vincent talked about Harry, more in generalities than in specifics. He was a good son. He liked to laugh. He loved having fun with his friends. "Of course, you've probably met his friends, especially the other Musketeers. They knew Harry so well. They must have told you lots of good stories about him."

Ardith took notes, but they didn't add up to much. Ruth answered all of her questions, but her Harry stories didn't reveal anything special. The Harry of Ruth Vincent's memory certainly didn't sound like the crazy kid that Eldon Reeble and his pals had talked about.

As the minutes went by and an hour passed, Ardith grew more and more worried. The interview wasn't helping her solve the mystery and it wasn't adding much she could use for a good human-interest story. Panic set in that she might not have enough to write a decent piece. Ruth's voice faded as Roger Hackford's grew louder: "Ardie, is this all we get from two days in southern Missouri?"

Then Ardith asked Ruth about the Boy Scouts. Her eyes teared up. "Harry never became an Eagle Scout. He came so close. He would have finished this summer."

Ruth stood up for the first time since the interview began and walked over to Harry's cherubic picture. "If only Harry had time to finish. If only he could have become an Eagle. That's what he wanted more than anything else in the world. It breaks my heart that he never knew what it was to be an Eagle."

As Ruth slowly shook her head, Ardith realized that she had her story: the unfulfilled dream of a little boy who most of all wanted to become an Eagle Scout. She didn't need anything more from the interview. Finally feeling a sense of calm, Ardith relaxed and began a real conversation with the disconsolate mother—just two women talking, finally with some degree of ease.

Ruth began asking questions, about Ardith's job, about her family, about college, about whether she liked working for the newspaper, about what she was going to do in the future, about whether there was a man in her life, and about whether she planned to have kids.

"How was your trip down to Matulia? Did you learn anything new about Harry?"

The question was so innocent, Ardith so at ease, that she didn't even notice she had started talking about the bump on Harry's forehead. Not until she became aware of the change in Ruth's eyes, the piercing pain unlike anything she had seen that day, did Ardith realize that she had inadvertently turned Ruth's life and her own upside down.

Ruth Vincent, the reluctant but gracious interviewee, turned into Inquisitor Vincent, the ferocious cross-examiner. Eyes intent on the only person who seemed honest with her about Matulia, Ruth pressed on.

Now on the defensive, Ardith tried to evade Ruth's increasingly probing questions. The bump on Harry's head grew with every answer. Recognizing, too late, what her off-hand comments had ignited, Ardith began to mimic Mike Maldeth, unconvincingly assuring Ruth that the bump had no connection to Harry's death. Like many skilled reporters, however, Ardith proved to be an uncomfortable interviewee.

Then, with unexpected suddenness, Ruth stopped and showed Ardith to the door. Still in shock over what her lowered defenses had unleashed, Ardith walked trance-like to her car.

As she drove to the *Tribune* office, Ardith began to compose the lead for her story, the loving son who had died without fulfilling his dream of becoming an Eagle Scout. But she knew she couldn't stop with that. By bringing up the bump on Harry's head, she had unwittingly forged an unspoken moral pact with the grieving mother.

· · · · · · · · ·

# CHAPTER 32

# FEATURE STORIES

Ardith wrote rapidly all that afternoon and well into the evening. Although she tried to write *the* story, she ended up writing *stories*.

She wrote the story of a fun-loving boy who enjoyed playing pranks. She wrote the story of a sweet young boy who wanted, more than anything else, to become an Eagle Scout. The stories of a grieving mother in a too-empty house, of a tragic accidental death, of a killing, and even of a possible murder. The story of a cover-up, although she wasn't sure what was being covered up, and of a conspiracy, although she wasn't exactly sure what the conspiracy was about.

As she finished each story, she clipped the pages together and put them in a neat stack, as was her habit. Soon she had a pile of stories. Someone could have picked them up, read them, and, except for the names, not recognized that they concerned the same people and the same events.

Ardith wasn't sure which of these stories was true. She wasn't sure if any of them were true. She began to doubt if there really was a truth. If there was, she wasn't sure how she was going to determine it and how she was going to tell it.

That night in her small, spare, one-bedroom apartment, free from the newsroom's rows of clattering typewriters, Ardith read and reread her stories in relative silence, trying to decide which one—or ones—she was going to give to Roger Hackford the next day. She poured herself a second glass of white wine, a taste she was just beginning to develop after years of beer in Waverly and Columbia.

Not until late that evening did she wrap her mind around the realization that only two readers counted. First, she had to please Hackford, who demanded good content and tyrannized writers about spelling, grammar, structure, and style. Fuzzy thinking and imprecise writing served as his archenemies. She had no choice but to satisfy him.

But there was now a more important reader: a slight, soft-spoken woman on Randolph Road who was grieving over the loss of her little boy, lamenting the fact that he had never become an Eagle, and, because of Ardith's big mouth, was now writhing with the knowledge that somebody may have been involved in her son's death, knowledge for which Ardith had to take full responsibility. If Ardith couldn't help Ruth Vincent, then what difference did it make if she pleased Roger Hackford?

When Ardith lay down late that evening, she could nearly recite each of the stories by heart. When she awoke around 5 a.m., she had decided what to do. As she lay there, she began recomposing the story in her mind, word by word, theme by theme, arranging and rearranging the sequence, conceptualizing each bridge from topic to topic until she had constructed it into a clear, compelling narrative. She had never written anything like this before at Mizzou or at the *Tribune*.

Ardith smiled, imagining Roger Hackford's grin as he proclaimed to the entire newsroom that her article was great and would be the front-page lead story, maybe with a two-column headline. But her smile quickly disappeared as she reimagined his face smirking and frowning before he called her over and asked her why she had written this piece of fantasized crap, a word he had never used with her but often shared with the guys.

Ardith got up, made herself a cup of coffee, carefully prepared her daily two pieces of toast with a light dusting of jam, and listened to the growing off-to-work traffic on nearby Evans Avenue. She hardly noticed the ballads being sung on her small, brown radio and, as she dressed, she couldn't remember if she had just taken a shower.

. . . . . . . . . .

# CHAPTER 33

# FEATURE STORY

*W̶ho killed Harry Vincent? That's right, killed, even though the story I wrote in 1948 said that he died in an accident.*

\* \* \*

Ardith tried to focus on her next assignment, but she couldn't refrain from glancing, over and over, at City Editor Roger Hackford, who nodded repeatedly but without a visible trace of emotion as he read her Harry Vincent story.

Writing that story had been a unique experience for Ardith. As always, she had wrestled with words, structure, and ideas. But this time, early that Friday morning, she also wrestled with her feelings, her conscience, and especially her sense of conflicting responsibilities to the *Tribune*, to Ruth Vincent, and, as much as she hated to admit it, to her still-frozen career.

"More than anything else in the world, Harry Vincent dreamed of becoming an Eagle Scout," read her lead. "Those dreams were shattered, along with the dreams of his family, when the always-happy, fun-loving fourteen-year-old from south Kaioga City died last week at Boy Scout Camp Matulia under somewhat mysterious circumstances."

Ardith watched with frustration as Hackford set her article aside while he talked to two young reporters, both men, who were probably being sent out to cover something urgent or at least important. That dance repeated itself twice more before

Hackford returned to her piece. A half hour or so later he gestured to her, initiating her long, excruciating walk over to his desk.

"Quite a story, Ardie. Quite a story. Maybe we'll run it on the front page. Depends on what else comes up, if there's not too much big happening. Probably next week."

"You liked it?"

"Of course. You did a fine job. That Eagle Scout hook—nice idea."

"The moment Ruth Vincent mentioned it, I knew it was the right angle."

"Here are my notes, Ardie," he said, handing her the marked-up sheets. "Give it a rewrite and let's see where we stand."

Ardith skipped back to her desk. After getting a new cup of coffee, she settled down for the finishing touches. Then she noticed the black lines eliminating three entire paragraphs. Hackford had scratched out all references to the bump on Harry Vincent's forehead as well as the "under somewhat mysterious circumstances" in her lead.

She pondered her strategy and decided to follow all of his recommendations except for the complete removal of the bump sequence. Instead, she tightened her discussion of the bump by including it as part of her description of the body and by removing the hint that it might be somehow related to his death. To no avail. This time Hackford uncharacteristically walked over to her desk.

"Still stuck on this bump thing, huh, Ardie?"

"I was just trying to describe his body as accurately as possible and that bump was kind of strange."

"Strange, how?"

"Well, he fell on his back, not on his forehead. So how did he get the bump?"

"How? All kinds of ways! Maybe he bumped into a tree or

hit his head going into the outhouse, I don't know. Look, there's no reason to include something that might rile people up when there's no evidence that it means anything."

"I just thought that…"

"Ardie, listen! We're not going to mess up a good story with far-fetched conjecture. That's it!"

The young reporter looked with dismay at her boss. She had never seen Hackford so adamant and unwilling to discuss one of her stories. Although always a tough and demanding editor, he usually showed patience when discussing a reporter's suggestions. This time his fixed gaze, almost a glare, made it clear that he wasn't going to budge and she'd better drop the issue if she wanted her story to be published.

"Look, Ardie. I admire your imagination. And you wrote a truly beautiful story. We just can't be insinuating that a sheriff and a county coroner don't know what they're doing or that they're involved in some kind of skullduggery. Sure, I know these Hexterville folks aren't the sharpest people around, but I've known Pug Jones for a long time. We've even done some scouting together over the years and he's a pretty good old boy. No reason to go out of our way to make him look bad."

Hackford took a deep breath and focused on the back of Ardith's eyes. "Ardie, you would like a front-page story, wouldn't you? It'll be your first one. I imagine there'll be others."

Ardith folded. Reluctantly, she deleted the forehead bump, which returned to its resting place as a sequestered detail in the coroner's report, soon to be forgotten by the few who knew about the reference. Forgotten, that is, except by Ardith Millett and Ruth Vincent. And, of course, it remained in the stack of stories resting on the small table in Ardith's cramped apartment, ultimately to be placed carefully in a large brown manila envelope labeled "Harry Vincent."

# THE BOSS

Roger Hackford was right. Ardith Millett had written "Quite a story." It ran on the front page of the *Kaioga City Tribune*, minus the bump and with only a single-column headline.

But readers found it, read it, and loved it. Some of them must have also cried about it, because the *Tribune* soon began receiving phone calls and letters. So did Ardith, whose desk phone rang for several days with compliments about her wonderful story and even some promises of "I'm going to read all of your stories from now on." Ardith also received a very nice, carefully handwritten letter from Ruth Vincent, thanking her for the lovely tribute to her Harry. Not one word about the missing bump.

Tux Harrison, too, was surprised by the number of parents who read the article and called him, saying the troop should do something for Harry. A couple of them even suggested that maybe the troop could make him an honorary Eagle Scout. Tux replied that he didn't have the authority to do anything like that.

But Andy Norcutt, The Boss, viewed things differently. The long-time head of the Kaioga City Area Council, The Boss often spotted opportunities when others saw challenges. Where Tux fixated on Scout regulations, Andy focused on action and public image. By the time the three Troop 64 leaders—Tux Harrison, Bill Perryman, and Ed Marshall—met with Norcutt in his office, The Boss had decided to act. He quickly made it clear that Harry Vincent was going to become an Eagle Scout.

"Look, fellows, we've got to move on this. Fast! The *Tribune's* getting all kinds of response to that girl's article. They're on board with us."

Actually, the *Tribune* was more than "on board." They were pushing it. As the managing editor told The Boss, "We helped you with this situation, now it's your turn to do something for us. It would be great if the *Tribune* got credit for contributing to the Vincent boy's memory and to his family's recovery."

"Tux, we're going to need letters…from all three of you. Strong letters about what a fine scout the Vincent kid was— popular, did so much for the troop. Stuff that National is going to like, that will convince them to make this exception for us. Stuff that we can read publicly when Vincent's folks receive his Eagle Scout badge at this fall's public ceremony."

Harrison wasn't about to challenge The Boss. Still puffed up with his conferred Matulia importance, Ed Marshall jumped in, congratulating Norcutt on his great idea and guaranteeing that The Boss could count on him to make it work. Perryman was another matter.

"Wait a minute, Andy," Bill objected. "Aren't we going a bit too far? We can't honor Vincent. We all know he was a lousy scout. In fact, we should have booted him a long time ago."

"Bill, this is a special situation, a very special situation," replied Norcutt. "Situations like this don't come around very often, maybe never again. We've got to act. We've got to show that the Scouts really care…and we do care. Maybe we'll even put up a plaque for Vincent at Matulia. Have a little ceremony. Get the *Tribune* down there to cover it."

"Yeah, maybe even build a statue showing him depantsing someone."

"Bill, shut the fuck up!"

Perryman knew he had gone too far with The Boss. He'd better quit while he had a chance. Before long, that overbearing little maniac might order him to perform an Indian dance in Vincent's honor.

So Perryman shut up and wrote his letter, as did Harrison and Marshall. And the three of them agreed to read their letters at the public ceremony where Ruth and Philip Vincent would receive their son's honorary Eagle badge. The National Boy Scout headquarters went along with Andy Norcutt's impassioned recommendation. The Boss had pulled it off.

. . . . . . . . .

# CHAPTER 35

# EAGLE SCOUT

*My* career was launched by a fraud.

\* \* \*

The Boy Scouts didn't put on a special ceremony for Harry Vincent or erect a plaque at Camp Matulia, but they did include a brief, dignified interlude during that fall's citywide Eagle Scout ceremony at which The Boss presented an Eagle pin and a special plaque to Ruth and Phil Vincent. All of the Hawks joined the Vincents on stage. Chucky Karlson, who was also receiving his Eagle, told a story about Harry, a story approved by Tux and The Boss.

Scouting was enormously popular in Kaioga City, so lots of boys were promoted at the semi-annual Eagle Scout ceremony, which generally drew a large crowd. The *Tribune* always covered it and usually ran a group picture of the new Eagles, often more than a hundred.

Publicity surrounding Harry Vincent's honorary award made that year's event a major citywide happening. The Vincents received a standing ovation from the overflow crowd, the largest in years for an Eagle Scout event. Following the ceremony, the *Tribune* ran a picture of a smiling, cherubic Harry Vincent dressed in his scout uniform. Roger Hackford made certain that Ardith Millett wrote all of the stories, starting with the Scouts' decision to make him an Eagle.

In the aftermath of Harry Vincent's ordination, the sudden-ly famous Ardith Millett accepted an attractive offer from the prestigious *Chicago Telegram.* But she stayed in touch with Ruth Vincent. Not often. Just a note between the two of them now and then.

# PART IV

# PARADE GROUNDS

. . . . . . . . .

# CHAPTER 36

# CHUCKY KARLSON

"Quick, everybody! Look over here!"

Chucky Karlson rolled onto his right elbow so he could see what Harry Vincent was screaming about. There, in the glare of Harry's flashlight, knelt big Duster Fertig, hunched over Vincent with Harry's dick shoved deep into his throat. Shocked by the sudden and undesired attention, Duster pulled away.

"You son of a bitch, Vincent!"

Harry broke into hysterics, soon joined by the four observant Hawks, whooping, hollering, and applauding. Having never before watched a blow job and certainly not expecting to witness one that night, Chucky stared with fascination. A sideshow that Chucky hadn't considered when the six Hawks decided to lug their sleeping bags out to the Parade Grounds to spend their second night of camp beneath the Matulia sky.

"OK, Vincent, it's your turn," snarled Duster, lowering his pajama pants.

"Bullshit. You didn't do it long enough."

"That's because you shined the goddamn flashlight on me."

"Well, I'm not blowing you until you finish."

The other four Hawks watched in awe as Harry and Duster argued, then negotiated, finally coming up with a compromise. Duster wouldn't suck Harry any longer and Harry wouldn't go down on Duster, but he agreed to jack Duster off until he came. Duster insisted that everyone shine their flashlights on

Harry, which they all happily did, watching with glee as Vincent polished off his big friend.

Afterward, Duster insisted they all swear not to say a word about this to anyone. Not just swear, but swear on Scout's Honor. Solemnly they all raised their three fingers and swore, first together, then one by one. Duster wasn't taking any chances.

The six boys lay back down, needing some sleep before another busy day of hiking, swimming, and taking merit badge classes. Chucky even had an evening astronomy class, where they would go out on the Parade Grounds and identify constellations, maybe even standing on the very same spot where the "Harry-and-Duster-Show" had just occurred. He chuckled at the thought.

The next morning Duster reiterated his threat. "Remember, you guys. You all swore under Scout's Honor. Not a word. Not one damn word."

As Flipper and Freddy headed back to the tent, Duster stopped the other three Musketeers. Pressing his thumb and forefinger together, he demanded, "Musketeers' Vow, all of you!" They raised their hands with their private sign. Grabbing Harry's shoulder, his giant fingers digging into Vincent's back, Duster muttered, "Especially you, asshole. One word and I'm going to kick the living shit out of you."

* * *

Predictably, Vincent began hedging on his promise almost the moment they got back to their tent. He didn't exactly break the Vow, but with Duster's back to him, Harry pursed his lips in the form of a suck and pointed at the big guy. Abruptly turning around, Duster spotted his sneering friend performing for fellow Hawks. When Duster took a step toward him, Harry threw up his open palms. "Hey, Duster, we promised we wouldn't say a word to anyone else. I didn't. And I won't, I swear!" Duster stopped, knowing he could only make things worse.

After that, Duster became fair game. Even Flipper Green joined in with a modest remark. "Shut up, greenhorn," threatened Duster, "or I'll dip your head in the lolly." When some of the other scouts came by and asked why they were howling, Foreskin Freddy put them off with a smirking "Oh, nothing," followed by another explosion of tent laughter. Soon Ed Marshall peeked into the tent and asked how things were going, igniting more unexplained hysterics.

* * *

On top of his other concerns, Chucky now had to deal with what had happened on the Parade Grounds. A taunting Harry Vincent. A furious Duster Fertig. A tentful of boys eager to share the juicy story with the rest of the troop but straining to keep silent according to their oaths.

Maybe these many distractions could help explain why Chucky had gotten caught by the lolly trap. A veteran camper should have known better, to always check for protruding knots before lifting the toilet lid. But Chucky didn't check.

Chucky decided he would find the culprit and beat the crap out of him. Well, depending on who it was. Not exactly a tough guy, the slender, skinny-armed Chucky wasn't about to mess with anyone like Earl Gregorio, who played fullback on the South Hills High football team. But Chucky didn't have to try out his detective skills. At the campfire that night, he heard Harry bragging about having gotten a full house with his lolly trap.

The next day wasn't fun for Chucky. It started raining again, making the steep camp grounds slippery, slick enough that he tripped and bruised his knee. He managed to capture a lazy black snake in Reptile Study, but Bird Study was going badly. With all of the stuff he was dealing with, Chucky hadn't spotted the required number of birds and the counselor had rejected his birdhouse. The rain clouds meant that they might not have astronomy that night. At this rate, he might not earn all of his merit badges, which would mess up his plans to make Eagle by fall.

The topper, of course, was the incessant "Shit-Face" from just about everywhere. Even his Bird Study counselor now addressed him as "Shit-Face Karlson." The only reason Chucky put up with all of this was his knowledge that he had earned this name, fair and square, and that in previous years he hadn't hesitated to use it for other outhouse miscreants. Still, it was getting on his already-fraying nerves.

Chucky made a crucial decision late that Thursday afternoon when he spotted Harry having a furious argument with Bill Perryman. Putz put his hand on Harry's shoulder—to calm him down, Chucky supposed—but Harry slapped it off. Harry was the only scout with the guts to talk back to the gruff adult leader and, for whatever reason, Perryman seemed to tolerate it. As he watched the confrontation, Chucky decided to have it out with Harry that day.

\* \* \*

The scarlet sun was dipping behind the forest that evening when the opportunity came. Chucky, Harry, and Flipper were alone in the tent after dinner when Harry announced that he had to go to the lolly. Chucky followed him.

"Harry, wait a minute."

"You heading for the lolly, too, huh? After all, that's your place," he snickered.

"No, I need to talk to you."

It wasn't a pleasant conversation. Chucky explained that he could deal with the lolly trap and being called Shit-Face. After all, he had been negligent, getting caught off guard. But he needed Harry's help with the other Hawks. The tent had spun out of control, and the two younger scouts had decided to imitate Harry, wising off and not cooperating. Duster was getting more and more pissed. Putz Perryman had threatened to remove Chucky as patrol leader.

Harry didn't seem to take Chucky's remarks seriously. "Hey, Chucky, you're making a big deal out of nothing. You know me. I'm just having fun. Duster can take a joke. And I've been doing my part in the tent." Harry paused for a moment. "Chill out. Everything's going to be just fine, Shit-Face."

One Shit-Face too many. Chucky's right fist clenched at that last remark. He thought about punching Harry's grinning kisser but held off, knowing this would mean the end of being patrol leader and maybe even becoming an Eagle.

"Is that all?" Harry snarled. "I got to go to the lolly."

With that, Harry abruptly turned away and continued down the path. Chucky watched as Vincent took the sharp zig to the left and disappeared behind the trees. Sort of disappeared, that is, because even in the deepening twilight Chucky could still glimpse him through the branches. He saw Harry stop, then spotted the back of Duster Fertig's giant skull. Their heads shook with increasing agitation. Then Duster's right arm came up, a rock in his hand.

"What's up, Chucky?"

Chucky turned at the sound of Trent Georgis.

"Oh, just kind of hanging out watching it get dark."

"Chucky, there's something I've been meaning to ask you."

Chucky felt like rushing down to see what was going on between Harry and Duster, but Trent was busy talking and Chucky didn't want to drag him into the middle of their argument.

Trent rambled on and on and on. By the time he finished and headed off toward the Parade Grounds, the lolly path had virtually disappeared into darkness. Chucky paused, trying to decide whether to go looking for Harry and Duster. Then he heard Terry Fleener's cries of "Oh, shit!" when he tripped over Vincent's sprawled, lifeless body.

\* \* \*

Chucky left Terry to watch Harry's body and ran up to the leaders' tent, where he found Ed Marshall. The adult leader instructed Chucky to block off the path and send Terry over to the health lodge, where he found the camp physician treating a kid who had cut himself with his Boy Scout knife. It didn't take the camp doctor long to determine that Harry was dead, but it took nearly five hours before the deputy sheriff and county coroner got out to the camp and ascertained the cause of death.

When the sheriff himself came out the next day, Chucky didn't tell him about Duster Fertig with the rock in his hand. He didn't feel he was lying, just not relating everything he knew. Sure, he could tell the sheriff about seeing Duster, but what could he say? That he saw him through the trees talking to Harry and then raising his hand with a rock in it? That's all. Trent Georgis had come along and distracted him. When he looked back, it was too dark to see anything. Only when Terry Fleener shouted did Chucky run down and find Harry's body.

What would happen if he told about Duster? He'd get his friend into lots of trouble. Duster might even get arrested. For what? Because Chucky saw him holding a rock? And if Chucky started talking, it could all come out. The night on the Parade Grounds. The razzing of Duster. Who knows what more? Maybe even the lolly trap. He could see it in the newspaper. He might even lose his chance to become an Eagle Scout. And for what? For telling them that he had seen Duster holding a rock? He hadn't seen him hit Harry.

Chucky didn't sleep much that night. He imagined himself calling the sheriff and telling him the truth, the whole truth.

Maybe he should. Maybe it was the right thing. But the rising sun melted his determination. He couldn't do that to Duster, who had brought him into the Musketeers. And his testimony probably wouldn't lead to anything except trouble for his friend and, of course, for him.

The story of Harry's death, which appeared in both the *Hexterville Sentinel* and the *Kaioga City Tribune*, and his follow-up obituary proclaimed what the sheriff and coroner had concluded: accidental death from a fall on the lolly path, although they used less colorful language to describe that twisting trail. The obituary ended Chucky's indecision. It was too late to say anything. He would look even worse now if he blurted out this new information because he'd have to explain why he'd lied and waited so long to change his story.

He also kept his story to himself that Sunday night when the Hawks met with the adult leaders. Even when Tux asked the dreaded question: "Look, is there anything more we ought to know? Have you told us everything, absolutely everything?"

Tux's direct question became Chucky's point of no return. He looked at the other four boys, especially the scowling Duster. Then he made his silent commitment to keep on with his story, a story that served a noble purpose, protecting his patrol mates and especially Duster, who probably hadn't done anything wrong except get into an argument with Harry and pick up a rock. Nothing more. At least nothing more that he had actually seen.

Glancing at Duster to reassure himself, Chucky made it simple: "That's it. We've told you everything. Absolutely everything. Right?" Duster affirmed Chucky's statement, followed by the others.

When Tux Harrison made them swear under Scout's Honor that they wouldn't spread any of these Harry stories, especially to the *Tribune* reporter, it simplified things for Chucky. Even more so after Tux's threat about his not becoming an Eagle. He had to be decisive. The next morning Chucky took charge with his patrol.

"Everything's going to be OK. The leaders don't want these stories getting out any more than we do. From now on, just keep everything to yourselves. We can only trust other Hawks. Does anyone want to say anything?"

The boys had said more than enough, way more than enough. They probably would have liked to cram some of those words back into their mouths. But those would be the last words they would utter at camp about Harry Vincent's escapades or their conversation with the adult leaders—not to other scouts, not to the shy, skinny girl from the *Kaioga City Tribune*, not even to each other. No breaking of Scout's Honor.

Later that day, Chucky's and Duster's eyes met silently across the water trough. After that, they didn't talk much or even look at each other.

· · · · · · · · ·

# CHAPTER 37

# DUSTER FERTIG

Duster Fertig knew he shouldn't have trusted Harry Vincent. But Harry had pledged Scout's Honor.

"Look, Duster. I promise. You go first and then I'll blow *you*. I swear, by Scout's Honor. It'll be neat. We'll be quiet. The others will never notice us."

The clouds cooperated, hiding most of the stars and the sliver of a moon. The other Hawks were busy talking and laughing. Then Harry's flashlight caught him in the eyes and he heard Harry shouting, "Quick, everybody! Look over here!" Duster stopped, but it was too late. By then everybody was howling.

"You son of a bitch!" Duster roared. Harry howled. Duster's fury was restrained by the knowledge that he'd get the last laugh by shining his flashlight on Harry when he reciprocated.

"OK, Vincent, it's your turn," he snarled.

"Bullshit. You didn't do it long enough."

Duster wasn't about to go down on Harry again. They argued in front of the awestruck audience of four. Finally realizing that he wasn't going to win, Duster decided on second best. "All right, Vincent. If you're not going to, then you've got to jack me off…with everybody watching…until I come."

A few enjoyable moments later, Duster's fleeting pleasure turned into panic. What if they tell somebody? Of course they would. Everybody's going to think he's a real dork. Duster knew his only chance was to swear the other Hawks under Scout's Honor. A husky, barrel-chested kid, he glared at them, his dark bushy eyebrows converging into a threatening V.

"All of you, make the Scout Sign. Now swear, all of you, that you won't say one word about tonight. OK now, one at a time, swear it!"

Their solemn oaths didn't help Duster sleep all that well. Watching the stars begin to peek through, Duster wished he had followed his instincts about Harry. "Make a wish upon a star." Like hell. That wouldn't do much good.

Duster shook Harry awake. "Listen, you son of a bitch. You say one word and I'm going to beat the shit out of you. I mean really kick your butt. I'll make sure you never get a hard-on again," he said, his fist pumping toward Harry's groin.

"Of course I won't say anything."

"You better not, asshole!"

The threat made Duster feel better, but he realized that his moment of triumph wouldn't last. Taking crap in the Hawk tent would be bad enough, but Duster knew the other shoe was going to drop. It did later that morning when Jack Brighton from the Snake Patrol asked him if he'd had fun on the Parade Grounds last night. Despite the seeming innocence of the question, Jack's smirk suggested he knew what had happened. But how? Duster seemed to recall Jack and Harry walking back together from breakfast. That son of a bitch Vincent! Scout's Honor doesn't mean one damn thing to him. Or even the Musketeers' Vow.

Jack Brighton wasn't the only kid who smiled at Duster that day. It seemed like everyone was smirking at him but not saying anything. Harry must have made them pledge Scout's Honor. They must have sworn not to tell Duster that they knew his juicy secret.

Then the big guy caught a break—the lolly trap. It got

Shit-Face Karlson right where he deserved, in the kisser. That's what he got for not standing up for his friend. Maybe the others would turn their attention to Chucky. But when Duster lay down for the night and heard Harry making a sucking sound, he knew he couldn't go on for ten more days like this.

But who could he talk to? Not Chucky. Karlson didn't have the balls to clamp down on the others. In fact, he was worse than the others because he was supposed to be Duster's great friend. After he had gone out of his way to get Chucky into the Musketeers. After all those times they had slept at each other's houses. Guess that didn't mean shit. That Merona hick hadn't proven to be much of a pal. Neither had moody Greg Brooks.

So it had to be Harry. But what could he say to him? Harry was having too much fun spreading his secret around the camp. Maybe he could beat him up. Even if he got kicked out of camp, at least he would have the beautiful memory of Harry's busted face. No, that wouldn't work. Then Harry would feel self-righteous and tell *everybody* about the Parade Grounds, maybe even the adult leaders.

Duster fell asleep, an uneasy sleep, thinking about the next day's conversation—or confrontation—with Harry. Waking up the next morning with a feeling of fierce determination, Duster looked forward to resolution. For the first time since the Parade Grounds, he even smiled.

\* \* \*

Duster stood alone at the entrance to Lola's Lolly. As the scarlet sun dipped behind the forest, he glanced up the hill at the Troop 64 compound. Even in the rapidly deepening twilight he could see Chucky Karlson and Harry Vincent arguing heatedly. Harry must have said something really crappy, because Chucky clenched his right fist and glared as Harry turned his back on him and began the descent down the lolly path.

# CHAPTER 38

· · · · · · · · ·

# GREG BROOKS

"Greg, I've got to talk to you…privately."

"OK."

Greg Brooks and Chucky Karlson climbed up to the Parade Grounds. Greg could see Orion, bright and sparkly.

"What's up, Chucky?"

"I need your help…with Harry. He's on a tear and I don't know what to do about it. I've asked him to lay off Benny and Freddy, but he just laughs at me. They're really upset. Now Duster's pissed at him, too, about the Parade Grounds."

"Maybe he needs the shit kicked out of him."

"Of course he needs the shit kicked out of him, but I can't. I'm the patrol leader. Would you say something to him? Let him know that I'm not the only one who's angry."

Greg stared up at the stars. He could see most of the Big Dipper.

"Let me think about it."

The next day, Greg was still thinking about Chucky's request when Harry started in again about Greg's sister and her boobs. No particular reason, just Harry being Harry, but this time it really pissed Greg off. The little prick better stop being Harry if he knows what's good for him.

\* \* \*

The scarlet sun was dipping behind the forest and the twilight was deepening when Greg heard Harry and Chucky shouting at each other at the top of the lolly trail. Climbing back up the hill from Lola's Lolly, Greg had just reached the first bend, so he couldn't catch every word through the trees. But he could tell Chucky was angry and Harry was flipping him off, like he flipped off everyone.

Greg relaxed for a moment, then continued up the trail. Hearing the crunching of pebbles from someone coming down the path, Greg stepped back into the trees. He watched as Harry rounded the turn and headed straight down the zig toward him.

# CHAPTER 39

• • • • • • • • •

# HARRY VINCENT

Harry Vincent flopped onto his back after he had serviced Duster, basking in the whoops of the other Hawks. He could hardly wait until he got back to camp so he could spread the word. But he hadn't counted on Duster's next move, demanding that they all swear, by Scout's Honor, not to say anything.

Yet Harry wasn't too concerned. He thought about the many times he had pledged Scout's Honor and ignored it. He was still wondering who he was going to tell first when Duster clawed his shoulder.

"Listen, you son of a bitch. You say one word and I'm going to beat the shit out of you. I mean really kick your butt. I'll make sure you never get a hard-on again," he said, his fist pumping toward Harry's groin.

Harry realized he'd have to be careful.

\* \* \*

For several minutes after they got back to the tent, Harry played it cagily. But with Duster's back to him, he couldn't resist. Silently signaling the others' attention, he pursed his lips and imitated a deep suck. Harry got just what he wanted—laughter, lots of it. He ignored Duster's infuriated scowl. Harry looked at Chucky to see if Mr. Patrol Leader was going to intervene. He didn't. Just a passive look of acceptance, signaling that he knew he couldn't do anything or maybe he didn't want to do anything.

Then Harry decided to test Duster's limits. As the funniest guy in the tent, maybe in the whole troop, he had to live up to his reputation. He decided on a baseline ethical code for following the Musketeers' Vow: He could say anything he wanted inside the tent, but he wouldn't tell anyone outside of the Hawks.

*Let's see.* If anyone else asked him about the Parade Grounds, he would simply grin and purse his lips. No words. That was his pledge. If he kept that up, maybe he'd trap one of the other Hawks into spilling the secret. Then he could verify the remark by merely smirking and making a sucking sound. Harry took pride in his honorable solution.

In Reptile Study and Bird Study classes that day, Harry made certain not to mention the sleep-out. The other Musketeers were in those classes, too, and Harry didn't want to feed Duster's suspicion, certainly not provoke his ire. So he focused on the differences between coral snakes and cottonmouth water moccasins. As the counselor explained that water moccasins had particularly limber jaws and could envelop a good hunk of human extremities, Harry couldn't help comparing this to Duster gagging when Duster had gone down on him. When he burst out laughing in the middle of the explanation, he hoped Duster wasn't on the same wavelength. That afternoon's Bird Study hike hadn't provided him with a similar analogy.

The day turned into hours of frustration for Harry. Except for the Hawks, not one damn person even hinted at knowing about the blow job. As darkness approached, he decided he needed to do something to vent his frustration. Looking down at Lola's Lolly, Harry decided on his course of action.

He grabbed a strong piece of rope, one of several he had packed for just such an occasion, and headed down to the lolly. Checking inside, he found only one grunter, Stewart Stein, a pudgy kid who was lousy at basketball.

Harry slipped behind the lolly, chose a good-sized rock, and tied one end of the rope tightly around it. The other end was already firmly knotted, which Harry had done carefully before packing the rope for Matulia. Waiting until the other scout had departed, Harry chose the middle seat on the uphill side of the lolly, carefully lowered the rock partway into the pit of horrors, and then closed the seat, securely anchoring the knot which would soon become invisible due to the darkness.

Harry climbed up through the trees, avoiding the lolly path. In about ten—maybe fifteen—minutes, he heard cries of anguish coming from the lolly. The multiple voices let him know that he had struck more than one butt, but it would be a few more minutes before the word spread that Shit-Face Karlson had caught it straight on.

At the campfire later that night, while Camp Director Rocky Reynolds was exhorting the boys to become more involved in community service, Harry shared his accomplishment with a couple of scouts, of course swearing them by Scout's Honor not to pass it on. Harry was on a roll. As soon as the usual lights-out jabber ended and the other boys in the tent began dozing off, he struck again.

"Duster's got a lot of suck," he muttered. When he didn't get any response, he fired again, this time louder. "Duster's got a lot of suck!" After a few moments of silence, Greg joined in: "Yeah, Duster's sure got a lot of suck." Pretty soon the whole tent, minus Duster, of course, had become part of the "lot of suck" celebration. Harry knew he had struck gold.

Then he upped the ante, chanting, "Duster's got a lot of, Duster's got a lot of, Duster's got a lot of…experience." Pretty soon the entire tent began chanting in unison. "Experience" had become the code word for "suck." Harry was delighted with himself.

The next day he tried out his new code word on the way to the mess hall for breakfast. Spotting Duster a few feet away, Harry began to chant, "Duster's got a lot of experience." Freddy joined in. Not one reference to "suck," Harry rationalized. That would be betraying both Scout's Honor and the Musketeers' Vow. More importantly, it might push big Duster over the edge.

As the day rolled on, the refrain spread. Other troop members began to chant it around Duster, even though they didn't know what it referred to. Only sourpuss Chucky Karlson wouldn't join in, maybe because of the lolly trap.

Sooner or later, Harry figured, someone would ask about this "experience" stuff and one of the Hawks, caught off guard, would forget the pledge and explain it. Then Harry would really become the camp envy—both a lolly trap grand slam and a blow job during the same camp session. Who knows what other honors he would accrue in the remaining days?

* * *

On the way back from dinner, Harry spotted Putz Perryman near the sloping path leading to the Hawk tent. *Obviously waiting for me*, he thought. Probably still pissed about the short sheets. No damn sense of humor. Oh, well.

"Hello, Mr. Perryman," he flipped off as he tried to walk past him. Perryman's hand clamped down on Harry's right shoulder.

"Vincent!"

"Yeah, that's my name."

"Vincent!"

"You're right again."

"Vincent," Perryman whispered, glowering at the scout. "Vincent, we need to talk."

"About what?"

"You know."

"If I knew, I wouldn't ask."

"Vincent, can you say one sentence without being a wise ass?"

Harry couldn't restrain himself from grinning at the frustrated adult leader.

"Vincent, I'd like the truth."

"I've told you the truth. I always tell the truth."

"Like hell you do!"

Harry looked at Perryman's hand, no longer clamping his shoulder, just resting softly on it, almost gently. Vincent stiffened. It wasn't the first time that son of a bitch had put his hands on him. Vincent twisted his body, then slapped Putz's hand away. The last thing Harry saw as he walked away was Perryman's shocked—make that, *furious*—face.

As he lay down for a few minutes after dinner, Harry felt nearly triumphant. Then he realized that in the heat of battle he needed to use the lolly.

* * *

The scarlet sun was dipping behind the forest and the twilight was rapidly deepening as Harry headed for the lolly path. Then he heard Chucky shouting.

"Harry, wait a minute."

"You heading for the lolly, too?" Harry asked. He couldn't resist grinning and adding, "After all, that's your place." He wasn't about to let Shit-Face Karlson forget about last night's lolly trap.

"No, I need to talk to you."

Chucky paused.

"Look, I need your help, Harry. With the Hawk Patrol."

Harry hadn't expected this. Why did Chucky need *his* help? He waited for Chucky to continue.

"Let me clear the air. I know about the lolly trap. Sure, I'm a little pissed, but I should have spotted it. That's my fault. And I can put up with being called 'Shit-Face.' So I'm not going to tell the leaders about it as long as you'll help me with the patrol."

*So that's what's happening*, Harry thought. *Chucky's trying to bribe me.*

Increasingly animated, Chucky went on. The tent was out of control, especially the younger scouts, who looked up to Harry and were imitating him. If he would be more cooperative, the greenhorns would be too, especially when it came to Duster, who was becoming more and more pissed—especially now that everyone was talking about his "experience." This had to stop.

Taking a deep breath, Chucky continued. He was also catching flak from adult leaders, especially Putz Perryman, who had threatened to remove him as patrol leader. Chucky nearly begged Harry to cooperate. Harry decided to stall.

"Hey, Chucky," Harry shouted, "You're making a big deal out of nothing. You know me. I'm just having fun. Duster can take a joke. And I've been doing my part in the tent."

Chucky seemed to calm down. He probably would have remained that way if Harry had known how to button his lip, but he didn't.

"Chill out. Everything's going to be just fine, Shit-Face."

Harry saw Chucky stiffen, his right fist clenched. Realizing he had probably pushed it too far, Harry decided it was time to go.

"Is that all? I got to go to the lolly."

With that, Harry turned away and continued down the path. He paused for a few moments just before the path zigged to the left. Maybe he ought to go back up and tell Chucky he'd be glad to help him. After all, they'd been friends for a long time. Oh, well, they could talk later.

Harry turned left and walked slowly. Still distracted by the conversation with Chucky, he didn't notice the figure hidden in the trees until he almost bumped into him.

"You son of a bitch," came the snarl.

"What?"

"You dirty little son of a bitch."

Harry saw the rock in the raised right hand. It came down hard on his forehead. The last thing Harry remembered was falling backward.

# CHAPTER 40

# END OF THE MUSKETEERS

After Ardith Millett's departure, a stillness settled on the Hawk tent and remained there for the rest of the session. No more joking and escapades. Conversations in the mess hall became agonizing until Ed Marshall split them up and assigned them to other tables. They all found new pool buddies.

For Duster Fertig, the last few days of camp became easier. No more leers from other scouts. No more taunts about his having "experience." Greg Brooks went about his business, while Benny Green and Freddy Collins enjoyed their respite from hazing, although they both missed Harry's fun. With everybody in the tent behaving and now with Ed Marshall's support, Chucky had reasserted his leadership. He could also concentrate on his merit badges, which he finished joylessly along with the two other Musketeers.

On a few occasions, the three Musketeers would sit down together quietly, saying nothing, waiting for someone else to start the conversation. It was as if they each had questions for the other two but were afraid to ask, fearing what answers they might receive and what lies that might require.

Soon after the troop returned to Kaioga City, the Hawk Patrol broke up. Chucky was promoted to the Lordly Lions along with most of the other patrol leaders. Tux Harrison found new patrols for Freddy and Flipper. Greg transferred to the troop that met at Jonathan Norwood Elementary School, while Duster dropped out of Scouts altogether.

The Musketeers stopped hanging out. They never sat together in class and tried to avoid eye contact whenever they passed each other in the school hallway. Even when they occasionally ended up at the same lunch table, they didn't talk much.

As the weeks dragged by, Chucky became more and more convinced that he had done the right thing by not telling about Duster. He still thought about Duster holding the rock. He'd probably always remember that. But he couldn't imagine getting his friend into trouble for something that probably hadn't happened. After all, he hadn't really seen anything, at least not much.

Duster became more relaxed as the blow job receded into ancient history. None of the other Hawks—ex-Hawks, that is—ever said anything to him about the Parade Grounds. That certainly wouldn't have been true had Harry Vincent still been alive. But Duster tried to stop short of feeling happy that Harry was no longer around to say anything.

The Musketeers had something else in common. When they were out and around—never together, of course—they avoided going past Harry's house. When Ruth and Phil Vincent came to the Eagle Scout ceremony to receive Harry's badge, Chucky and Greg shook their hands and promised to come by soon for a visit. They never did.

# PART V

# GOLDEN GATE

• • • • • • • • •

# CHAPTER 41

# BATTLE PLAN

Since receiving the letter from Ardith Millett Cunningham about her new book, Charles Karlson, M.D. thought of little besides their upcoming meeting. The Harry Vincent incident was going to end up in print. When it did, Karlson, a noted San Francisco physician and prominent member of Bay Area society, would almost certainly be part of the story. But what story? What was she after?

Karlson had always taken pride in his methodical approach to problems, an approach that had helped him as he made diagnoses and conducted delicate surgeries. Because of his skill in weighing evidence and developing insights that many others missed, other physicians often called upon him to consult and lawyers liked using him as an expert witness.

Recalling the summer of 1948 meant unleashing long-dormant emotions, but Karlson struggled to maintain his poise. *How can I get things exactly right after thirty-six damn years? Focus, you son of a bitch.* Karlson carefully outlined his battle plan on a white ruled pad.

I. Reconstruct those days at Matulia as clearly as he could.

II. Decide and rehearse what he could and could not tell her.

His mind raced through memories of Matulia days. Harry Vincent had certainly pissed off plenty of people. Duster Fertig on the Parade Grounds. Short sheeting Putz Perryman, ragging Greg Brooks about his sister, pounding Greenberg on Benny Green, and depantsing Foreskin Freddy Collins in the shower.

III. Learn as much as he could about Ardith Cunningham.

Charles had already visited the San Francisco Public Library and came away impressed. She had become a well-known journalist, popular columnist, and author of three other books. This didn't fit with his image of that shy, skinny, flat-chested reporter, but he had better prepare for a more formidable cross-examiner.

IV. Read the articles she had written for the *Kaioga City Tribune* in 1948. But he would have to get them without drawing attention to himself. For now, back to the list.

V. What questions might she ask? Three stood out.

1. How *well* did you know Harry? Obviously.

2. What can you tell me about the day he *died*? Of course.

3. When was the *last* time you saw Harry?

The surgeon remembered *that* all too clearly. Harry arguing with Duster Fertig. Duster lifting the rock. Trent Georgis interrupting him as he watched. Chucky looking back at the empty zig in the lolly path where Duster and Harry had been arguing. Racing down after he heard Terry Fleener scream, "Oh, shit!" Seeing Harry lying on his back, not breathing. Summoning Ed Marshall.

Was he really going to tell her the truth? After all of these years of hiding the truth, at least part of it? Chucky's hand shook as he wrote the next item on his ruled pad.

VI. After thirty-six years, why had Ardith Cunningham decided to write a story about some kid she didn't even know who happened to die at a Boy Scout camp in 1948?

Maybe she suspected something. That Harry didn't just die, that someone else may have been involved, and now she was trying to find out who and what and how and why. That Cunningham woman wasn't just an interviewer. She was the enemy.

Charles Karlson picked up the phone to call Renata Antonini.

# CHAPTER 42

· · · · · · · · ·

# FALSE STARTS

*We all live with regrets, regrets about things we did that we wish we could go back and do over. Unfortunately, we can't. But sometimes we are given the opportunity to atone for those mistakes. One of those I'm-sorry moments was a story I wrote in 1948 when I was a young reporter just starting my career at the Kaioga City Tribune.*

\* \* \*

Ardith Cunningham re-read her latest attempt at an introduction, one of many she had written over the years. Always fastidious, she had dated each unsatisfying effort, placed it in a manila folder marked "Vincent Introduction," and returned it to her filing cabinet of future projects. One of these days she would complete that story.

Now that day had come. She had signed a contract for a new book, *Unfinished Stories*, a revisiting of journalistic pieces she had published during her rich career. The first such piece would be about Harry Vincent and how she had bungled the story, failing to tell the whole truth.

\* \* \*

*I got my first big break in 1948 while I was a reporter at the Kaioga City Tribune. My City Editor, Roger Hackford, asked me to write a human interest story about a young Boy Scout named Harry Vincent, who had died that summer at*

*Boy Scout Camp Matulia in southwest Missouri.*

*To this day I can visualize my trip to Camp Matulia — the steamy weather because of so many rains, the gravel road into the camp, the dusty paths among the tents, and the bright faces of so many young men enjoying their stay in that beautiful natural setting.*

*I remember regretting the way that I had dressed, particularly the heels that made it so difficult to . . .*

\* \* \*

*I screwed up my first big assignment, screwed it up badly. It happened while I was a young reporter at the Kaioga City Tribune in 1948, when I wrote a feature story about a young man named Harry Vincent, who had died that summer at Boy Scout Camp Matulia in southwest Missouri.*

\* \* \*

Ardith shook her head in frustration. She had to find the right introduction. She tried again, as she had done so many times before.

\* \* \*

*Women have never had it easy in the newspaper world. Maybe that helps to explain — not excuse — something I did at the beginning of my career.*

\* \* \*

*I know a veteran journalist shouldn't begin a story by saying I'm sorry. But I have to. I am sorry, terribly sorry, about the first big story I ever wrote. It happened in 1948 while I was a young reporter, not long after I had graduated from the University of Missouri.*

\* \* \*

*If I had H. G. Wells' time machine, I would go back to 1948 and redo the first big story I ever wrote, the story that launched me on my journalistic career.*

\* \* \*

Too detached, Ardith thought. Too clinical. Too damned pompous. She banged her fist on the desk.

\* \* \*

*Above all, journalists should have courage and honesty. Unfortunately, I began my career by being a coward and a liar. It happened during my first full-time professional job at the Kaioga City Tribune.*

\* \* \*

*I began my journalism career by selling out. I sold out when my editor said he wouldn't run a story the way that I wrote it. Thinking only about my career, I caved in and changed the story to make him happy, to make certain I kept getting good assignments, to keep my job.*

\* \* \*

*An apology is not a good way to begin a story, but it's what I have to do. I messed up my first big assignment, the story with which I won my first major journalism prize. I didn't tell the truth, at least the whole truth, because I didn't have the courage to stand up to my editor. Now I have the opportunity to finish that story.*

\* \* \*

Maybe she was being too hard on herself. It's just an introduction, a damn introduction. She needed to move on with the story. But how? Ardith thought of the Vincents.

\* \* \*

*A devoted mother suffered, suffered greatly, when her son died under mysterious circumstances in 1948 at Boy Scout Camp Matulia in southwest Missouri. Because of my personal weaknesses, I unintentionally and inexcusably added to her suffering. I was wrong then; now I'm going to try to make it right.*

\* \* \*

*Who killed Harry Vincent? That's right, killed, even though the story I wrote in 1948 said that he died in an accident.*

\* \* \*

*My career was launched by a fraud.*

\* \* \*

Ardith had contacted many of the people she planned to interview. Most important, she had written to Ruth Vincent, almost hoping that Ruth would write back and ask her to drop the story, that she had already suffered enough, that another version would serve no purpose except to increase her pain. A letter that would lift Ardith's burden of not having fulfilled an unspoken debt to a grieving mother.

But Ruth's letter didn't lift that burden. In fact, it made it heavier. Ruth Vincent was happy to meet with her. She would do whatever she could to help with the story. Her boy Harry deserved the full story. Ardith looked vacantly at her typewriter, then poured herself a glass of Chardonay.

# CHAPTER 43

• • • • • • • • •

# RENATA ANTONINI

Renata Antonini was one sharp cookie. Karlson had met her while testifying as an expert witness in a big medical malpractice case, where she served as private investigator for the defense. At the victory cocktail party, he and Renata had chatted at length. "If you ever need a good private investigator, Big Man, here's my number," she had whispered into his ear as she slowly slid her card into his right front pants pocket. Now he needed her.

Ted Seagram, the lead attorney in the case, had rhapsodized about Renata's skills. "She's more like a magician than a snoop. Ask for some document, she'll produce it. If she can't, you can be pretty damn sure nobody else can either." As Ted explained, Renata seemed to be part of some clandestine syndicate, where people from all over the country (maybe the world) took pride in helping each other find deep dark secrets and incriminating evidence.

When Karlson met with Renata, she laid down the ground rules. "I don't want to know why you want what you want. Just tell me what you're looking for, give me enough information to get started, and I'll see what I can do. Oh, one other thing. No asking me how I got the stuff. Agreed?" She didn't want to be burdened with how's and why's.

Karlson wanted everything he could get on Ardith Cunningham. Some of the stuff might be difficult, especially the coroner's report. He told Renata that the last thing he wanted was for anyone to know that he had suddenly become interested in what a hayseed coroner in a Southwest Missouri hick town had to say about the death of some pimply faced Kaioga City Boy Scout thirty-six years ago.

As the weeks passed, Karlson's concern grew. Maybe Renata hadn't been able to pull it off. When she finally called and said she was ready to meet, he felt both relieved and queasy.

Renata always dressed invisibly and made certain that her hair and makeup attracted minimal attention. Not attracting attention had become part of her arsenal. But even such understatement couldn't hide the fact that she was a striking woman. Karlson had to strain to make sure their relationship remained strictly business.

She opened her nondescript briefcase, taking out three books and a large manila envelope full of documents. "This thing took some doing," she said, waving one of the documents. "You owe me one."

"Ardith Cunningham's been a busy lady. Three books. A popular columnist. A highly successful attorney husband. Two kids who have graduated from college. And she even knows you."

"What?" Karlson asked, badly feigning surprise.

"Check out page seventy-seven of *Small Town Girl.*"

He flipped to the page. There he was.

Chucky Karlson, leader of the Hawk Patrol, and the other Hawks didn't seem to want to say much about Vincent. Strange for a bunch of boys who had spent so much time together, shared a cramped tent, and helped each other with their merit badges. It seemed as if they had something to hide. Maybe they were afraid of something.

Karlson noticed Renata eyeing him as he read. Trying to be nonchalant, he even joked about Cunningham's hypothesizing, but he knew he couldn't put anything over on Antonini.

Karlson took the stuff out of the envelope. A copy of a faded photograph of Harry Vincent's body. A slew of clippings from the *Kaioga City Tribune*. An article from the *Kaioga City Inquirer*, the city's weekly scandal sheet: "Would You Trust the Boy Scouts with *Your* Son?" Bingo! A copy of the Green River County coroner's report, badly typed, as could have been expected. A much cleaner report, written by Renata, giving the highlights of Ardith Cunningham's life.

"You did well, young lady."

"I aim to please, Big Man," a term she had bestowed on him during the medical malpractice trial. He hoped she didn't use that name for other clients, although he felt like a jerk for being jealous.

After Renata left, Karlson flipped through the newspaper stories. "Kansas City Boy Dies Before He Fulfills His Dream" by Ardith Millett.

The article was filled with stuff that brought back memories: Harry's body; a description of the lolly path (she didn't call it that); a few quotes, including one from him (*"He was a great guy," said Hawk Patrol leader Chucky Karlson, who was in charge of the tent where Harry slept.*); even a mention that he and Benny Green had been the last people to see Harry when he left the tent to go down to the outhouse. But most of the article was about Harry's greatest dream—that he would earn his Eagle Scout pin and that he had been studying bird and reptile lore at camp to complete his requirements.

Unprepared for the emotion of the moment, Karlson choked up as he read the article. That bitch can write. No wonder the Scouts decided to make Harry a posthumous Eagle.

Then, in the middle of the story, Karlson spotted an ominous sentence: *According to the Green River County Coroner, Vincent died from a blow to the back of his head caused by his fall.* "ACCORDING TO THE CORONER." Maybe that was

Millett's way of saying that this was just the coroner's conclusion and there might be more to the story.

There were several other articles about Harry, all with Ardith Millett's byline, mainly concerning the Scouts' decision to award him an honorary Eagle pin at the fall ceremony. Finally, one published two days before the ceremony. It seemed pretty standard: "150 Scouts to Become Eagles," but the subhead read, "Dead Boy's Dream Fulfilled." Ardith Millett had become Harry Vincent's official chronicler.

Then Karlson turned to *Small Town Girl*, Ardith's memoir. She had devoted an entire chapter to Harry Vincent. Actually, just a few pages about his death, including Karlson's pro forma quote. Most of the chapter described how that event had launched her career. Her feature story—the one that had prodded the Scouts into making him an Eagle—had been picked up by other newspapers and had caught the eye of an editor in Chicago. Within a year, she had joined the *Chicago Telegram*.

The chapter was mainly a personal diatribe. Ardith's frustration at being given only mundane writing assignments at the *Tribune* while her male colleagues got juicy stories. Being sent down to Matulia on what she figured was a wild goose chase. Being stunned by the rugged beauty of Camp Matulia and becoming fascinated by the circuitous, tree-submerged, Z-shaped path from the Troop 64 encampment down to the outhouse, the path on which Harry had died.

Then there was her trouble getting a decent interview. The adult leaders seemed to clam up. The Hawks wouldn't say much more. Finally came Ardith's visit to the coroner's office. Harry had died from a blow to the back of his head, caused by falling. But he also had a large bump on his forehead, which couldn't have been caused by a fall on his back. When she tried to pursue the bump with the coroner, he blew off her questions, far too casually to really be casual.

Karlson pulled out the coroner's report and faded photo of Harry's body. There it was. The bump on Harry's forehead. He imagined Duster Fertig's arm coming forward, smashing the rock against Harry's face. He skimmed the report to see if there was anything more. There didn't seem to be, but the bump was enough. Then it was back to Ardith's chapter, how she had included her suspicions about the bump in her feature story, only to have that section deleted by City Editor Roger Hackford.

*This was one of the things in my career that I most regret: that I didn't fight harder to keep the bump in the story. I knew it was important. I still know it. I guess I was just too young, too female, too obsessed with my career, and too fearful of losing my first real newspaper job. But it taught me a lesson.*

Although her feature story had galvanized public support for the idea of awarding Harry his Eagle badge, Ardith seemed almost ashamed that the story had also given her national visibility, which led to the Chicago offer. Even though the Vincents had tearfully thanked her for what she had done for their son, she felt remorse for not pursuing the bump and exploring the reasons for the wall of silence. The chapter's last paragraph riveted him.

As much as I hate to say it, the tragic death of that young boy gave an unexpected boost to my career. But I'll never stop thinking that I didn't get the full story. Someday it needs to be told. Harry deserves that. His parents deserve the truth.

So that's it, Karlson muttered. For whatever reason, Ardith Cunningham still feels some sort of moral obligation to the Vincents. This had become a bigger challenge than he had expected. Cunningham didn't just want to finish a story; she was desperately pursuing atonement.

· · · · · · · · ·

# CHAPTER 44

# RETURN TO RANDOLPH ROAD

To Ardith Cunningham, the two-story house on Randolph Road looked pretty much like it had in 1948. Except it seemed smaller. She shook her head at how thirty-six years could play tricks with memory.

Pausing before she rang the doorbell, Ardith momentarily rued the fact that she hadn't visited Ruth since then. *Damn it,* she thought. *I could have come by at least once.* Written more often. She owed that to Harry's mother. After all, she had lost a son, her only child, and later her husband. And it was Harry's death that had jump-started Ardith's career, got her out of Kaioga City.

Ardith watched incredulously as a slight form opened the door. Was that Ruth? She seemed smaller, too. Almost tiny. Still pleasant, still reserved, still unremarkable. Barely smiled. Why should she? After what she's been through. After what Ardith had helped put her through.

"Please come in, Ardith."

The living room seemed tighter, too. Tighter and still dim. The single lamp with a nearly lifeless bulb, probably forty watts, sixty at most. To help you sit down, but not to read. Only to stare. The photograph was still there, Harry's photograph, sitting on the same small cherry upright piano tucked into the alcove. The sheet music still open, probably to the same Chopin étude.

But two things had changed. A framed newspaper article on the wall, Ardith's newspaper article, "Dead Boy's Dream Fulfilled." And an Eagle Scout pin sitting on a small, almost matching cherry cabinet, lovingly displayed against a light aquamarine velvet background.

"Won't you sit down, Ardith? Can I get you some tea?"

"Please, thank you. A cup of tea would be nice."

"I'll be back as soon as I put on the kettle."

The ritual began. The awful ritual. For a moment, Ardith wasn't sure why she had come. What could Ruth add? What could Ardith ask without causing Ruth Vincent more pain?

The ritual continued. Carefully poured cups of tea. Lifeless cookies. Sipping and hungerless munching. Of course, heavy silences while Ardith grappled for exactly the right words, the words that weren't there thirty-six years ago when she awkwardly tried to explain about the feature story she was going to write, when she mentioned that she wanted to do justice to Harry, when Ruth skewered her with "Justice? What's justice when my little Harry is dead? Last week I sent him down to scout camp. He came home dead. How can there be any justice in that? You can't write justice!"

This time there will be justice, Ardith vowed.

"It's nice to see you again, Ardith. I never had a chance to fully thank you in person for the lovely articles you wrote about Harry. The Eagle ceremony was so...it was so...busy. We didn't have an opportunity to really talk. I thought I might see you again, to talk privately, but then you left town so suddenly."

Why in the hell hadn't she come by, thought Ardith. At least once. Before she fled to Chicago. Just once. That would have been the right thing to do. That would have made today so much better, easier.

"You don't need to thank me, Ruth. I was just trying to do my best for Harry…and for you. He earned his award. I'm glad he got it."

"No, Ardith, he didn't get it," Ruth delivered a gentle, not-quite-bitter rebuke. "Harry never knew he was an Eagle Scout. It breaks my heart every time I think that he never had the opportunity to wear his Eagle pin. He was so close."

"That's not your fault. You did your best." Ardith paused. "But I didn't."

Ruth seemed perplexed. Or maybe not.

"You didn't? But your articles were so nice. And you won those awards. Now you're so famous. My friends loved your book. Would you mind signing my copy?"

Ruth walked across the room to the cherry cabinet and picked up her copy of *Small Town Girl*, nestled against the framed Eagle Scout pin. Ardith wasn't prepared for this. What should she write? Her hand began moving. "To Ruth, Affectionately, Ardith Cunningham" emerged on the title page, inappropriate, cold, savage.

Ardith silently pleaded with those mindless, mechanical words to disappear so she could start over, but it was too late. This whole thing was too late. Thirty-six years too late. She should have visited Ruth Vincent again back then, but she had been too obsessed with her articles, with making her escape from Kaioga City.

"Thank you, Ardith." Ruth almost smiled. "You've had quite a life…since you left Kaioga City."

Ardith couldn't say to her that "quite a life" was because of Kaioga City, because of her boy. She had moved on to bustling Chicago while Ruth tended to her barely lit sanctuary. That wasn't Ardith's fault. But the untold story was. The visit had become a disaster, but she had to press on.

"Ruth, I wrote you that I'm working on a new book." The words came abruptly.

Ruth inspected her before she answered. "A new book? About what?"

The journalist paused. She had explained this in her letter, so Ruth must know why she had come. Maybe she had forgotten. Or maybe she wanted Ardith to say it aloud, why she had decided to disturb Ruth's solitude after more than three decades of silence.

"The book is going to be called *Unfinished Stories.* It will be about stories that I wrote, to meet deadlines, so I didn't have time to, you know, get more detail. Get to the bottom of things. The whole story. Working for a daily newspaper, we seldom have the chance to get the whole story. New events keep happening. New assignments, new deadlines. Our stories are always so incomplete."

Ruth's eyes spoke puzzlement, concern, trepidation, maybe fear of the unknown.

"But you wrote about Harry's story in your book. Are you saying that you are going to add to it? You're not going to change Harry's story, are you?" uttered the suddenly distraught mother, as if Ardith were about to desecrate her treasured and fiercely guarded memory.

For a moment Ardith considered junking the whole idea of rewriting Harry's story. Maybe just let the legend rest, the story in the frame on top of the cherry cabinet, the modestly expanded but still wretchedly incomplete story in *Small Town Girl.* Let them lie quietly, undisturbed by the pursuit of more truth. But she couldn't. Ardith had to complete this journey, a journey she had been pondering for years.

"I'm not going to change Harry's story. I'm just going to add to it," she lied, knowing that some of her new insights might well tarnish Ruth's memory, a memory with which she had made peace, maybe.

"So that's why you're here?"

"No," Ardith lied again, hoping Ruth wouldn't reread her officious letter. "I was going to be in town doing research for the story and thought it would be nice to see you again, see how you are doing."

Ruth replied with bite. "I'm doing OK."

But Ardith was planning to disrupt OK. She watched her interview plan shrivel up, her questions probing for details, the questions of a prying journalist, not a consoling friend.

"There's one thing I really don't understand," Ruth continued. "Why did Harry's friends stop seeing me? You know, the Musketeers. They used to spend so much time in our home, with Harry."

Ruth had brought Ardith back into the game. Ruth didn't know it, but that was one of the reasons that Ardith had come, to find out about Harry's friends. And Harry's enemies. Anything that could help her figure out what might have led to that bump on Harry's forehead.

"That *is* surprising, very surprising. You mean they never visited you after they got back from camp?"

"Let me try to remember. Chucky Karlson came over right after camp, twice, I think. Gregory Brooks, once. Duster Fertig, never. But after the Eagle Scout ceremony, they stopped completely. All of them."

Ardith looked at the frail woman, afraid to ask direct questions that might shut her down. But she could tell that Ruth was preparing to go on.

"I remember those conversations. I remember them well. Strange, awkward, incomplete."

"Incomplete?"

"Yes, incomplete. I wanted to remember my boy. I wanted to know about his last day. What he did at camp that summer, how he looked, who he played with. I wasn't there to see his last day. The Musketeers were. But they wouldn't say much.

They wouldn't say much of anything. I asked Chucky. I asked Greg. Over and over. Tell me about Harry's last day, the last time you saw him, what he was doing, what he said. What were his last words? But I couldn't get them to talk. I tried. I tried very hard."

Ruth pondered the floor. A different Ruth, a knowing Ruth, looked up at her inquisitor.

"Maybe that's why they stopped coming by. Maybe they were tired of my questions. Maybe they were tired of talking about Harry. Maybe they couldn't stand to be around me anymore."

Ardith stared at Ruth Vincent, abandoned by Harry's supposed best friends, those little shits. They had damn well seen Harry on his last day, but they wouldn't tell her about it. Maybe because of what had happened that last day, they couldn't tell her. Ruth's wailing hardened Ardith's determination to extract those memories from the so-called "Musketeers."

"Ruth, I'm going to try to interview the Musketeers. I want to write the story of Harry's last day, the complete story. That's a gift I owe you."

Ruth's presence crystallized Ardith's journey, the journey she had to take. She just hoped the journey wouldn't crush the fragile woman in front of her. As Ardith got up to leave, she knew she should put her arms around Ruth Vincent. Just once before she left. But she couldn't. Or wouldn't.

# CHAPTER 45

# CALL FROM A FRIEND

After his last patient had left, Charles Karlson, M.D., went to the front desk to pick up his mail and phone messages. He spotted the receptionist's scrawled note. It was a call from an Aaron Fertig in Scottsdale, Arizona.

Aaron Fertig!!! Duster Fertig!!! After thirty-six years? His best friend until, back in 1948, when they couldn't be best friends anymore. If only Chucky hadn't glanced down at the lolly path. If only Trent Georgis hadn't interrupted him. Then he could have seen Harry and Duster waving goodbye and maybe even Harry tripping and falling. Then he could have told the whole truth about that late afternoon. Then he and Duster could have gone on being friends. They could have played golf. Maybe their families could have gone on trips together and he wouldn't be worrying about this bitch from Chicago.

Karlson waited until everyone had left before calling Duster. A man answered.

"I'm trying to reach Aaron Fertig."

"Speaking."

"Aaron, this is Charles Karlson… Chucky."

After a long pause, Duster proceeded, almost formally.

"Thank you for calling me back, Chucky. How have you been?"

"Fine, Duster. How about you?"

"Fine here, too. It's nice living here in Phoenix. No more Kaioga City winters." Duster paused. "Chucky, we need to talk. I suppose you've heard from Ardith Cunningham."

"Yes, I did."

"She also contacted Greg Brooks. He's living in Los Angeles."

"All of the Musketeers? I mean, all except Harry. She wants to talk to all of us?" Karlson breathed deeply. "Duster, I think we've got a problem."

"I know what you mean, D'Artagnan."

Chucky felt good hearing that Musketeer name.

"Porthos, we need to talk. The three of us. Before Cunningham interviews us."

"Greg agrees."

"You've talked to him?"

"Yes."

"Where shall we meet?"

"I could fly out there. Either L.A. or San Francisco works for me. For Greg, too."

"We could meet at my office, Duster. It's empty on Saturdays and Sundays."

"Sounds good to me. I can tell Greg."

"Do you two want to stay at my house?"

There was a long silence as Duster pondered his offer.

"Thank you, Chucky. Let's just meet and talk. I think that would be better."

Duster was right. It would be better. No idea how the conversation would go. If it didn't go well, it would be awkward if Duster and Greg were staying with him.

"What day can you come up?"

"How about next Saturday? Not this coming Saturday. The one after that."

"Fine. I'll clear my schedule."

"We can get early morning flights. How about 1 o'clock?"

"Perfect. Do you have my office address?"

"Yes. It wasn't hard to find. You've done pretty well for yourself."

"Yeah, life's great here. Look, I'll bring in some lunch. Do you like Chinese?"

"Sounds good." Duster paused again. "I appreciate your taking the time. It's very important that we talk."

"Yes, this whole thing is disturbing. Very disturbing. All of this digging into our pasts."

"I'm glad we'll be able to talk about things. Just the three of us, together." Duster paused. "It's been a long time. Too long. It'll be good to see you, Chucky."

"Yeah, Duster. It will be."

By now neither of them could bring himself to offer any more pleasantries. They both waited for the other to say goodbye. One of them did.

As the phone clicked, Karlson found himself envisioning all kinds of scenarios, none of them particularly good. What could the three of them tell her? Certainly not the truth. They would have to agree on lies. But what lies?

All because Harry Vincent had pissed off so many people. All because he, Chucky Karlson, had tried to protect a friend. All because some Chicago cunt gets a burr up her ass and wants to write a story about something that happened thirty-six years ago.

The sun was setting behind the Golden Gate Bridge, but today he didn't give a damn.

# CHAPTER 46

# VISIT TO ED MARSHALL

Ardith Cunningham didn't expect Ed Marshall to break down in tears. She hadn't come to Kaioga City to make him cry. Maybe to squirm a little bit. She wasn't trying to ruin anyone's life. Just trying to discover the truth, write the truth, tell the story, the whole story, finally.

For Ruth Vincent. Ardith paused and, for a moment, let total honesty seep in. For herself.

But Marshall did cry. He sobbed. This accomplished professional. This bald-headed stub of a man. This sniveling would-be molder of future leaders.

"That was my first full session as a troop counselor at Camp Matulia. And my last. I just wanted to help the boys, help them learn, help them grow up. I believed in the Scouts. I still believe in the Scouts. Everything I did was for the good of the Scouts. For the good of the boys. I wish I had stayed home. I wish I could..."

"Look, Mr. Marshall, I know you meant well. You gave up two weeks of vacation time to help the boys. Precious time. Time you could have spent with your own family. I respect your intentions. I really do."

"If only I had gone down some other year. Why that summer? That summer." Marshall shook his head.

"Mr. Marshall," Ardith said in a softer voice, "I'm just trying to find out what happened at Matulia. About Harry Vincent.

Before he died. After he died. I just want to be able to tell the whole story, accurately, honestly, completely."

Ardith couldn't imagine writing an entire chapter about adult men crying. She sat silently, waiting for Marshall to pull it together. His crying subsided. He sloppily pulled a wadded white handkerchief from his back pocket and wiped the tears from his eyes and cheeks.

"I'll try to help you, Mrs. Cunningham, but it's hard." Marshall's head shook, almost imperceptibly. Ardith couldn't tell if it was his Parkinson's. "It happened so fast, Mrs. Cunningham. It happened so very fast."

"What happened so fast?"

"They kept telling me what I had to do."

"Who kept telling you?"

"Tux Harrison. He was the head of our troop's adult leaders. Bill Perryman, the other leader. He didn't like Harry, really didn't like him. Rocky Reynolds, the head of the camp. He told me I had to take charge because he didn't trust either of the others. They all kept piling on me. Do this, Ed. Ed, you can't say this. Ed, The Boss wants this. Ed, you've got to lie. You owe it to the Scouts. I didn't have a chance to think it through. There wasn't time to think it through."

"So you're saying that it was all lies?"

"Not all lies. We told the truth, mostly. I told the truth. Just a few things I couldn't talk about. For the good of the troop. For the good of the Scouts. Mrs. Cunningham, you've got to understand. I was trapped."

Ardith watched Marshall plead to his basement den's hardwood floor. He finally stopped and looked up at her, his red eyes begging for redemption, maybe the kind of redemption Ardith craved.

"Please, Mrs. Cunningham. I'm not a bad person. I was just trying to do what everyone expected of me. I wish I could do it over. I would do it so differently. I promise. I swear to you. I've been a good citizen. I've been a good neighbor. People respect me."

Ardith let his words hover.

"You can't do it over, Ed. What's done is done. But you can tell the truth now. The whole truth. It'll make you feel better, knowing you've finally told the truth."

Ardith paused as Marshall wrestled with that quaint idea, the idea of telling the whole truth. Then she applied the clincher.

"Ruth Vincent deserves it. She deserves the truth."

Marshall took a deep breath, wiped his eyes again, and then looked at her like a twelve-year-old at confession.

"OK, Mrs. Cunningham. Can I call you Ardith? I'll tell you everything, everything I know."

Marshall looked at her again, begging, pleading. She gently nodded.

"I promise, Ardith. I'll tell you absolutely everything."

For a moment, Ardith almost didn't want him to tell her everything. Then she sat back, smiled cautiously, and allowed Marshall's words to gush forth, while she took copious, voracious, lacerating notes on her yellow lined pad.

# CHAPTER 47

• • • • • • • •

# REUNION

For whatever reason, Karlson felt greater dread about the reunion with Duster Fertig and Greg Brooks than he did about his upcoming interview with Ardith Cunningham. Maybe it was because he knew that she would grill him. But Duster and Greg? He had no idea what to expect, particularly from Duster.

They would have to come to some agreement about what to say about Camp Matulia. The truth? Harry's death? The Parade Grounds? Scout's Honor? Impossible. They would have to try to agree on lies.

Karlson methodically reconstructed Harry's final evening on his lined pad.

    ***The scouts come back from dinner.

    ***Chucky talks to Harry and Flipper Green in the Hawk tent.

    ***Harry leaves to go to the lolly.

    ***Chucky follows Harry.

    ***He and Harry argue (Flipper hears them).

    ***Harry heads down the lolly path.

    ***Chucky waits, trying to decide what to do next.

    ***He looks down to where the lolly path bends through the trees.

    ***He sees Harry and Duster arguing.

    ***He sees Duster raise his hand with a rock.

\*\*\*Trent Georgis interrupts him and they talk.

\*\*\*He looks back, but Duster and Harry are gone.

\*\*\*He hears Terry Fleener scream.

\*\*\*He runs down and finds Harry dead.

\*\*\*He leaves Terry with Harry's body and runs up to the adult leaders' tents.

\*\*\*Ed Marshall comes down and sends Terry to the health lodge to get the camp doctor.

\*\*\*The doctor goes back to the health lodge to call the sheriff.

\*\*\*A sheriff's deputy and the coroner come out to the camp.

Karlson tapped his pen. Did he miss anything? Yes. The most important thing. He didn't see Duster hit Harry with the rock. Or have the opportunity to see the two of them walk away after their argument. Now Ardith Millett Fucking Cunningham was trying to reconstruct the story, to tell the world how Harry died, and maybe even point the finger at someone.

He looked at his watch. If their planes landed on time, they ought to be getting here pretty soon. He fidgeted with the boxes of Chinese food that he had picked up on the way to his office, now laid out neatly on his conference table. Then he re-organized them, not once but twice, glancing repeatedly at the wall clock with its relentless pendulum.

The ringing of the intercom jolted Chucky from his house-keeping. After telling the concierge to send the gentleman up, Chucky went out to meet…whomever. When the elevator door opened, a middle-aged man stepped out. Chucky didn't recognize his face, but his broad shoulders and barrel chest said it was Duster, an even bigger version than he remembered.

"Hello, Chucky."

"Hi, Duster. Come on in."

Not a "good to see you" passed between them.

"You've got a very nice office, Chucky. And a beautiful view of the bridge. How long have you been here?"

"Actually, I moved to San Francisco right after my residency. Nineteen years now. How about you?"

"I'm an engineer. Been with Motorola in Phoenix about as long as you've been in San Francisco."

They looked at each other, unsure of how to proceed. Chucky pointed at the table with the Chinese food.

"You must be hungry after the flight."

Duster nodded.

"At least you probably don't have jet lag," Chucky said, trying to make a joke. Duster didn't smile but quietly sat down at the table. They looked at each other, awkwardly.

"Do you ever get back to Kaioga City?" they said at just about the same time, eliciting wry smiles. It also gave them something to talk about, something to take up time. Soon they were exchanging information. How they both still had family in Kaioga City and got back there every year or so. How the city had changed, yet hadn't. New buildings. Same hamburger joints. Former golf courses replaced by housing tracts. Modern homes. Old attitudes.

They both agreed on the last point. They also agreed that they would never again live in Kaioga City, although they enjoyed going back for short visits and still loved the beautiful fountains and rolling hills.

Chucky couldn't wait any longer. "Do you ever see any of the old gang, Duster?"

"You mean the Hawk Patrol?"

"I guess so."

"No, I haven't seen much of them since...since Matulia."

Chucky knew he meant since Harry's death.

"I haven't either."

"It'll be good to see Greg Brooks."

The two stared at each other through the numbing silence, both knowing the day had nothing to do with being "good to see" anyone. The intercom broke their silence and rescued them from continuing their impossible small talk. Chucky made his way back to the elevator.

Greg looked somewhat like Chucky remembered him, but skinnier, maybe even slight. He didn't smile. But solemn Aramis didn't smile all that much even when he was young.

"Hi, Greg."

"Hello, Chucky," Greg said, his voice rising slightly as if it were almost a question, as if thirty-six years had blurred his memory or because Chucky had changed so much as to make him unrecognizable.

"Duster's already here."

Greg and Duster shook hands with the same listlessness of the earlier encounter. Greg soon joined Duster in pawing the Chinese food.

"Have either of you talked to Flipper Green or Freddy Collins?" offered Chucky, stalling off the inevitable. The other two shook their heads.

"Freddy died," interjected Greg.

Duster nodded. "Well, they weren't Musketeers." He paused. "We certainly were. The 'Four Musketeers' always stuck up for each other."

Now that Duster had opened the door, however inadvertently, Chucky decided that it was time to enter.

"We sure did. Until that summer at Matulia."

Duster nodded again and repeated Chucky's offering, pausing after each word, as if to let it reverberate until it stopped echoing: "Until…that…summer…at…Matulia."

Chucky couldn't wait. "Duster, I'm sorry."

"For what?"

"For not standing up for you after, you remember, after the Parade Grounds. For not trying harder to keep the others from razzing you."

Duster looked pensively at the Kung Pao chicken.

"I sure was pissed at you, Chucky…and you, too, Greg. More than at Freddy and Flipper. They weren't Musketeers. And especially at Harry. He caused the whole damn mess. That's why I…"

Chucky couldn't believe that Duster might be about to tell them about the rock. He had to cut him off.

"Duster, I never told anyone. Nobody! And I'm sure not going to tell Ardith Cunningham."

Duster squinted, slowly shook his head, then broke into a half-smile. "Why would you think of telling Ardith Cunningham? Did you really think about describing the blow job I gave Harry? Are you still that much of an asshole?"

"Of course not, Duster. I've never told anyone about the Parade Grounds. Not at Matulia, not after we got home, not ever. Not my folks. I haven't even told my wife."

For the first time, Duster actually laughed. "Tell your wife? I can just see you telling your wife. 'Yeah, I looked over and there was Harry Vincent with his dick in Duster Fertig's mouth.' She'd love that one. I can hear her reaction, 'Oh, how interesting! When do I get to meet your nice friend Duster?'"

"Leave my wife out of this!"

"You're the one who mentioned her."

"OK, let's drop it. I didn't tell anyone about the Parade Grounds. I didn't tell anyone about anything."

By now Greg Brooks was in hysterics. Doubled over with

laughter and red in the face, he looked like he was about to choke. Chucky couldn't recall seeing Aramis laugh like that when he was a kid.

"Porthos," added Greg, "Just to clear the air. I'm not going to tell Ardith Cunningham about the Parade Grounds either. Your secret's still safe with me."

Silence settled in again, as the Musketeers helped themselves to Hunan beef. Maybe the broccoli would calm things down. Chucky couldn't figure out how they had gotten off on that tangent. They hadn't come this far to talk about the blow job or Chucky's wife.

The three men began reminiscing about Matulia. For a few minutes, it was diverting. Buddy check at the swimming pool. Funny things at campfires. The crappy mess hall food, especially the beans. Those awful pre-breakfast Bird Study merit badge hikes when the counselor would point to a tree and say, "There's a purple-chested sparrow," and they would all nod and agree they'd seen it, even when they hadn't, and dutifully write it down on their bird recognition forms until they reached the required fifty sightings.

They giggled at those memories, yet all the while knowing they hadn't gotten together to talk about purple-chested sparrows. Chucky finally decided to get to the point.

"Guys, you flew all the way to San Francisco, for a reason. We've got a problem. We all have to talk to Ardith Cunningham. We all have to tell our stories. At least part of our stories. About the night Harry died."

Duster stopped laughing and took a deep breath before speaking. "Do you remember that night?"

Greg raised the ante. "How could I forget it? I remember everything that happened that night, as if it happened yesterday. How about you, Duster?"

"I was standing at the bottom of the hill, next to Lola's

Lolly," said Duster in a low voice. "I looked up the hill and saw Harry arguing with you, Chucky. I mean really arguing. You looked totally pissed, as if you wanted to slug him. When I went in to take a crap, you were still screaming at Harry. When I came out, I couldn't see either one of you. A few minutes later, Terry Fleener yelled when he found Harry's body." Duster paused, then resumed. "Chucky, you were the last person I saw with Harry before they found his body...and you had your fist clenched, as if..."

Chucky sat dumbfounded. Duster in the lolly when Harry died? Duster seeing his argument with Harry? What next?

"Duster, is that what you're going to tell Ardith Cunningham?"

Duster paused and took a sip of tea before answering. "No, Chucky. Of course I'm not going to tell her. I haven't told anyone. That's one of the reasons I had to talk to you today. I wanted you to hear it from me, face to face. I've never told anyone about your argument with Harry and I won't. But I do want to find out what happened."

"Wait a minute, Duster," said Chucky. "Let me get this straight. You saw me arguing with Harry. But what did *you* do after we split, when Harry started down the lolly path?"

"Chucky, I didn't stay until the end of your fight. I couldn't. I had to take a crap. When I came out, I didn't see either one of you."

"Duster, this is complete bullshit. *You* talked to Harry *after* our argument, on the way down to the lolly. I know you did. I saw you!"

"You saw *me*? What do you mean, you saw me? That was the last time I saw Harry, while you were threatening him. I never saw him again, alive."

"Duster, I *saw* you. I looked down and the two of you were... arguing...through the trees where the lolly path zigs. I saw you pick up a rock and…"

"Wait a minute. You saw ME? How in the hell could you see ME? I wasn't even there."

"Duster, I saw you. It was getting dark, but I could see Harry's face and the back…" Chucky's voice cracked when he heard himself saying "back." Over the years, he had rerun the story hundreds of times, but somewhere along the line "back" had faded from his internal narrative. Now there it was. He had seen the *back* of Duster Fertig's head. He had never seen his face!

"Duster, are you telling me that you didn't go up the hill, meet Harry at the zig, and argue with him there?"

"Hell, no. When I came out of the lolly, I couldn't see either one of you."

"But you must have seen Harry's body on the way up."

Duster shook his head.

"I didn't go back up the lolly path. I took the shortcut up the other hill to see some guys in the Antelope tent. I didn't know anything about Harry until I heard Terry screaming. When I learned what happened, all I could think about was you arguing with him."

"When I saw the body," Chucky said desperately, "all I could think about was you threatening Harry with a rock. But I didn't tell anybody. I swear to God. I never have. I lied to the sheriff. I lied to the adult leaders. I've lied to everyone. You were my buddy. You were a Musketeer. I knew if I told them what I saw, you'd be in all kinds of trouble."

"Chucky, you didn't see *me*. I saw *you*! Why do you think I didn't tell anyone about *your* argument with Harry? I didn't want to get *you* into trouble."

The two men sat silently, the sound of the pendulum growing louder. Greg broke the deadly silence.

"Guys, I was there, too. I was coming up the lolly path and I saw Harry coming down. Then somebody stepped out of the trees and started shouting at Harry. I stopped. I don't know why. Then he swung at Harry. I think he was holding a rock. I froze."

"Who was it?"

"Yeah, who was it?"

Greg smiled, sort of, and waited, looking back and forth between the other two.

"I don't know. It was almost dark and there were trees in the way. I couldn't see who it was."

Chucky and Duster looked at Greg, half believing him, half believing each other.

"One other thing, guys," Greg added softly. "I was a Musketeer. I *am* a Musketeer. I would never say anything that could hurt another Musketeer. I've never told anyone about the Parade Grounds or what I saw on the lolly path the night Harry died. I promise. Not anyone. And I won't tell Ardith Cunningham."

Chucky crossed to his desk and came back with a bottle of Bushmills Irish Whiskey.

"Would you like a glass?"

"Thanks, Chucky. I could really use it."

"Me, too."

The three men sat silently, pondering the day's revelations, trying to make sense of that awful evening, thirty-six years ago. It was like looking into a funhouse mirror, twisting your body and face into all kinds of distortions. Except it wasn't any fun. Duster broke the silence.

"Thanks, guys, for not saying anything about the Parade Grounds. I mean it."

"And thanks, Duster, for not telling about my argument with Harry," whispered Chucky. The sense of how much he had missed his old friends suddenly enveloped Karlson. As he looked at the sagging hulk and the frail old comrade, their youthful features began to emerge. "You two have been real friends. You've *always* been real friends. And, Duster, I will never say a word, to anyone, about seeing you threaten Harry with a rock…what I thought I saw."

The three men sipped their whiskeys, thinking about how each had held the others' lives in their hands for three decades. The Musketeers had fought, back to back, to keep Cardinal Richelieu's men at bay. Now they had to face their next adversary, an avenging angel from Chicago. One of them had to ask the next inevitable question. Chucky did.

"Duster, if it wasn't you, who did I see with Harry? Who did Greg see? The one holding the rock."

Duster shook his head. "I guess we don't know who that other guy was. We'll probably never know unless Ardith Cunningham figures it out. Lots of people were pissed at Harry—the three of us, Flipper Green, Foreskin Freddy Collins. Who knows who else? Especially Putz Perryman. He looked like he wanted to kill Harry the night of the Boy Scout Roundup. And after the short sheeting that first night at Matulia."

The Musketeers burst into laughter at the mention of Harry's repeated handiwork.

"Harry was really something," offered Greg in a low voice. "There'll never be another Athos."

The three sat in silence as Chucky quietly refilled their glasses. Duster finally broke the ice.

"We know one thing: It wasn't one of us. And we don't want to say anything that might make Cunningham think it was."

Greg jumped in. "I don't think we ought to say that we saw anything…nothing about anyone arguing with Harry or hitting him. We didn't see anything, right?"

The three nodded with resignation.

"We know one other thing, guys," added Chucky, staring at his friend. "We've all been protecting each other for three decades, even though it meant lying over and over."

"Yeah, Chucky, and lying under Scout's Honor."

"But we kept the Musketeers' Vow."

Chucky turned to Greg. "And you, Aramis. I didn't see you on the trail. This is the first time I've heard your story. Whatever you saw, you didn't say anything about me or Duster. You've really been a friend. You're a true Musketeer."

It was time for another of those long silences that had become a major part of their reunion. Duster again broke the logjam.

"Chucky, why didn't we tell each other about this way back then? Or you, Greg?"

Chucky took a deep breath. "Because we couldn't, Duster. We just couldn't. That's probably why we stopped seeing each other." Greg nodded as Chucky continued. "Maybe because we were all afraid, to say, to suggest out loud, that one of the others might have killed Harry?"

"Afraid?" Greg asked nobody in particular. "You're probably right, Chucky. We were all three afraid. That must have been what happened. After that day, I don't think I could have hung around with you and joked and laughed and double dated or whatever, knowing one of you might have killed Harry. We all knew it, didn't we, Chucky? We all knew we couldn't be friends anymore. Not with what we saw. Not with what we thought. We couldn't even say we can't be friends anymore. We couldn't say anything, not to each other, not to anyone else."

Chucky refilled the glasses. The Musketeers sipped their drinks, waiting for one of the others to ask the inevitable. Greg, the thoughtful, pensive Aramis, came to the rescue.

"What do you think Ardith Cunningham is going to ask? Is

going to write?"

Duster wearily exploded.

"At this point, I don't give a damn. She can write whatever she fucking wants. She can tell about the blow job. She can say the three of us conspired to kill Harry because we were all pissed at him. Do your worst, Cunningham. I'm too tired to care."

A smile crossed Chucky's face. "And while you're at it, bitch, be sure to explain our motives. Duster didn't get his blow job and I got whomped by Harry's lolly trap. What good will your book be without old Shit-Face Karlson?"

"Don't leave me out," Greg jumped in. "Harry never let up on my sister. Never!"

The three men were now laughing uproariously.

"What will the Scouts say if she writes about all of that camp stuff?"

"They'll probably be pissed that we told her, even though we swore we wouldn't under Scout's Honor."

The laughter finally subsided, broken periodically by a guffaw provoked by who-knows-what memory. The three drank in silence and dabbled with cold Chinese food.

"Guys, would you like to stay with us tonight?"

Duster smiled pensively. "Thanks, Chucky, but I think I'll take a rain check. I've got too much on my mind. I'm going to try to catch a late plane home. If not, I'll stay near the airport and get an early flight out tomorrow."

"Me, too, D'Artagnan."

"I missed you guys. I hope we see each other again soon."

"We sure let a lot of years slip away."

"We've got to catch up."

"Maybe we'll get together and have a good laugh about Cunningham's book after it comes out."

"And with our wives. They'll get a big kick out of it, too."

"Yeah, Duster's got a lot of…experience."

The three friends looked at each other with the calm joy of rediscovered friendship, a joy that did battle with the recognition of loss of more than three decades of camaraderie. Yet behind that joy lay thoughts, thoughts that could not be fully dismissed. The upcoming confrontations with Ardith Cunningham. And, even during this afternoon of honesty, the lingering suspicion that one of them, maybe all of them, was still holding something back.

As Chucky poured a final glass of Bushmills, a common thought pervaded the room. Despite their bravado, the Musketeers had not come to an agreement on the truth. And they cared very much—very, very much—what Ardith Cunningham would ask and write.

· · · · · · · · ·

# CHAPTER 48

# VISIT TO MIKE MALDETH

The Hexterville coroner's office looked even more drab than Ardith remembered from that soggy summer of 1948. It had been remodeled, but hardly improved. New flooring, new windows, new furniture. More modern, but tawdry.

Yet Ardith hadn't driven all the way down just to critique office furnishings. She was determined to confront that duplicitous county coroner—make that, *retired* coroner—who had refused to explain his report on Harry Vincent, especially the glaring reference to the large red bump on his forehead.

Mike Maldeth had lost his swagger, at least the swagger that she recalled from three decades ago. He seemed less imposing, almost squat. Maybe because Ardith was more mature, more erect, more confident. She'd been around. Interviewed high-flyers in plush surroundings. Also plenty of has-beens in places that never were, places like where she came from, places like this.

"Hello, Mrs. Cunningham. Welcome back to Hexterville," came the insincere greeting. "I guess you can see that things haven't changed much down here. But we did remodel the office. We've even got a nice little conference room where we can talk privately," he added, gesturing proudly to a cramped, nondescript glass enclosure toward the rear of the main office.

Ardith eyed the scratched-up table decorated with cigarette burns and the cracked, decaying imitation leather chairs. So this is what qualifies as a conference room by Hexterville standards. Not to mention the rancid smell of years of relentless nicotine, the small-town smell she detested.

"I don't want to take up too much of your time, Dr. Maldeth. You must be a busy man," Ardith responded.

Busy? In retirement, he probably doesn't do much more than guzzle beer, smoke cigars, and watch reruns of *The Real McCoys*.

"Always have time for visitors, Mrs. Cunningham. We believe in hospitality down here."

Ardith tried to take a deep breath as Maldeth sank into the sagging oversized chair at the head of the table.

"Let me get to the point, Dr. Maldeth. I have one real question. How did Harry Vincent die? How did he *really* die?"

"Well, Mrs. Cunningham, that was a long time ago. Lots of people die down here," he said, punctuated by a stupid chuckle. "I don't have all that much recollection of the Vincent case."

"How many people die at Camp Matulia, Dr. Maldeth? Especially from an unexplained blow to the dead."

"It wasn't exactly unexplained. I put the explanation in my report."

For several seconds she eyed the paunchy, bald prevaricator in the soiled tan shirt. "Dr. Maldeth, let me be blunt. Your explanation back then was nonsense, pure nonsense." She wanted to add, "You're pure nonsense, too," but held back.

Maldeth's eyes widened or receded. She couldn't be sure which, as if it made any real difference. He obviously wasn't prepared for such directness, especially from a woman.

"When I visited your office back in the summer of 1948, I asked you several questions, but you lied to me. I was only a neophyte reporter, but it was obvious that you were hiding something...something important. I'm going to be brutally honest. I'm very disappointed that you're still hiding it."

"Please, Ardie. Calm down."

Ardie! Maldeth called me Ardie, she gulped, trapping the

words at the base of her throat. Nobody calls me Ardie. Nobody has ever called me Ardie except that pig City Editor Roger Hackford, who muzzled my story.

Ardith Cunningham envisioned the conversation between Hackford and Maldeth. Hackford must have telephoned Maldeth and told the coroner about her. He probably talked to the sheriff, too, that Lester Jones, the one they referred to as "Pug." Hell, maybe Hackford talked to them *before* her visit to Hexterville. Referred to her as "Ardie."

The veteran journalist quickly reconstructed the trap they had set. Hackford had sent her down to do a soft human-interest story about Vincent's death. But to cover his butt, their butt, everyone's butt, he must have warned Jones and Maldeth so they could get their stories straight, get their lies straight. Hackford had set her up. He figured Jones and Maldeth could manipulate shy, little, inexperienced Ardie Millett.

But Hackford had been dead wrong. She had figured stuff out, stuff he didn't expect. When he realized what she had learned, what she suspected, the inconsistencies about Harry Vincent's death, he had to castrate her story. Ardith knew she should have fought for her story. But she was too intimidated by Hackford, too worried about her job, her career.

Ardith eyed the disgusting, wide-eyed little man cringing before her. She decided to get tougher.

"OK, Maldeth, let's quit playing around. You're not dealing with any 'Ardie.' You're dealing with Ardith Millett Cunningham, who is working on her fourth book," she said as she slammed down a copy of her book *The Pursuit of Truth.*

Maldeth picked up the book, inspecting it with a face full of amazement. Or was it trepidation? Putting the book down gently, he stared at the table for what seemed like an eon. Silence had become Ardith's ally. She waited for him to lift his shrinking head so that she could make eye contact.

"Here's the situation, Maldeth. I'm writing a book called *Unfinished Stories*. I'm devoting an entire chapter to Harry Vincent, how he died, and how his death was covered up." She paused to peer into his doleful eyes. "How *you* helped cover it up. You are going to be prominent in the story." She paused again to let her threat sink in. "So you've got two choices, just two."

"First, preferably, you can be honest with me, totally honest, and come out looking like a confused young man who was placed in a no-win situation, was under big pressure, and made a foolish mistake way back then by covering things up. An older and wiser man who has decided to make amends by telling the whole truth now. A basically good man who repents of his folly."

Ardith wanted to give Maldeth plenty of time to contemplate the attractiveness of this escape route, so she got up and walked over to the institutional grey wall with its fading photographs of Little League teams and the local Lions Club. When she looked back, Maldeth's mouth was ajar. It was time for the clincher. She stepped directly in front of him.

"Or you can keep up this nonsense about not remembering Harry Vincent and how you already explained his death. But if you do, I'll make your phony death report reek so badly that you'll come out looking like a serial liar, still lying. I've already got plenty of evidence to do just that. Plenty of stuff about the cover-up, the conspiracy between you and Pug Jones and Roger Hackford…and the others."

Ardith knew she should stop right there and let Maldeth wallow in those two dreadful options. But she couldn't. Thirty-plus years of suppressed ire rose up inside of her, thirty years of memories of Ardie Millett being patronized and pushed around by man after man. Now all of that ire focused on this little nothing in front of her. She had waited too long to hold back.

"It's completely up to you…numbnuts."

# CHAPTER 49

# DUEL

Charles Karlson, M.D., tried to envision Ardith Cunningham's questions, all perplexing, and his answers, all inadequate. Several times he imagined himself lurching for the phone and calling the bitch, telling her he was damned if he was going to be interviewed. In one of his dreams, he managed to dial her number, but then someone began pounding on his door, smashing it down while he vainly tried to get up and run.

After his last patient left, he picked up a *Sports Illustrated*, trying to read until she arrived. "A Mrs. Cunningham is here to see you," came the receptionist's call. Chucky contemplated putting on his suit coat draped over the back of a chair, then decided he'd go casual. Maybe he'd look more sympathetic. Loosening his tie and adjusting it under his vest, he sauntered down the long hallway, past the offices of his partners, and stepped into the reception room.

His first surprise came when that shy, flat-chested little girl turned out to be an erect, handsome, confident woman. Come to think of it, he probably didn't look much like the same timid Hawk patrol leader, the insecure transplant from Merona. He stared at the figure who was threatening everything he had built since those unsettling Kaioga City days.

"Hello. I'm Charles Karlson."

"Ardith Cunningham. Thank you for taking the time to talk to me."

The pleasantries continued predictably as they walked down the long hallway and he showed her his office with its view of the Golden Gate Bridge. He decided not to sit behind his desk but to join her in the complementary plush red-leather chairs. His patients, many city socialites, loved the poshness of his office. It made them feel as if they had chosen the right doctor and probably helped them accept the sticker shock of his bills.

Finally came the inevitable. "I know you're a busy man and I don't want to take up too much of your time," Ardith ventured as she took out her notepad. She had thought about asking him if she could use a tape recorder but decided it might make him become too selective about what he said. She wanted his words to come out naturally, irrepressibly, unable to be reswallowed. She focused on Chucky and his temporary insecurities, took a pen from her purse, then carefully put it down in front of him, making a display of nonchalance about not taking notes. Her first words were not what he expected.

"You sure did some crazy things in the Scouts back then, didn't you?" Ardith smiled gently, but knowingly. "Look, I've already talked to a number of your friends, so I've got a pretty good fix on those Matulia shenanigans."

Ardith looked down at the list on her pad. "Let's see, I've interviewed Terrence Fleener, Benjamin Green, and Gregory Brooks. Your fellow Scouts. Also Edward Marshall, one of your troop counselors. Alfred Reynolds, the camp director—you knew him as 'Rocky.' Michael Maldeth, the coroner who certified Harry's death. And others, including Ruth Vincent, Harry's mother. I also spent quite a bit of time with Aaron Fertig. You used to call him 'Duster.' I'm not sure if you've got much more to add, but if you do, that would be nice."

Ardith paused, her veteran interviewer instincts telling her that she had lowered Chucky's defenses by suggesting that his interview might be superfluous. She went on.

"Lots of folks have died. Andrew Norcutt, the Boss of the Kaioga City Scouts. Two of your troop leaders: Lloyd Harrison and William Perryman, the one the Hawks called 'Putz.' Sheriff Lester Jones, who investigated Harry's death. Even one of your Hawks died recently: Frederick Collins. I believe you called him 'Foreskin Freddy.'" Ardith paused. "I imagine I've got just about all I'm going to need unless..."

Chucky's mind was racing. She seems to know everything. What more did they tell her? Especially Greg and Duster. About Harry? About that last evening on the lolly path? Did the two of them stick to their agreement?

Ardith smiled, almost like a grandmother. "Boys will be boys, I suppose. I guess I'm kind of glad I've got two girls. They can't grab each other's nuts in the swimming pool."

In the face of this onslaught of knowledge, Karlson's carefully prepared responses had become useless. Did the Hawks hold anything back? Is there anything she doesn't already know? Unready for this, he groped for a counter.

"That's going to be quite a chapter, Mrs. Cunningham."

"I hope so. Most readers won't know what a lolly trap is."

There it was. "Shit-Face Karlson" would be in her book. He shook his head and tried to buy time by making light of it.

"I haven't thought about lolly traps in thirty years. You've really got some juicy stories."

Ardith proceeded with her well-crafted misdirection strategy to lower Chucky's guard. "Yes, but I'm not sure how many of them I can write. Look, you've probably read my book. *Small Town Girl.* You know what Harry and Ruth Vincent meant to my career. This is all still very painful for her. She wants the truth about Harry's death, but maybe she shouldn't have to face the *whole* truth. I don't want to taint her memories of Harry."

Chucky found himself feeling a little sorry for Ardith. Not

much. Just a little. "I understand. I guess that's part of your job…and mine. We hear lots of stories that we can't pass on." He felt like he might almost be out of the woods.

Ardith made a motion as if to put her pen into her purse, then hesitated. "There's one thing I'm still a little puzzled about. You were the Hawk patrol leader, and you and Aaron Fertig were great friends. Why didn't you make more of an effort to stop the rest of the patrol from making fun of him about the…blow job?"

In all of his preparations, Chucky had not expected to be grilled about that night on the Parade Grounds. He sort of grinned. "You know just about everything, don't you."

"Well, not everything. But I do know about the Parade Grounds. Mr. Fertig told me and Gregory Brooks confirmed it. How Harry tricked Duster. You all pledging Scout's Honor that nobody would say anything. Also the Musketeers' Vow. It's funny. Once Aaron started talking, he seemed to want to get everything off his chest." Ardith paused. "Do you?"

Karlson felt at a loss. If Duster wanted to get things off his chest, did he tell her everything? What about Greg? He wasn't sure which way to go.

"I should have done better," Chucky said softly. "You're right. Duster was my best friend. He's the guy who welcomed me in when I moved from Merona. I should have stood up for him. But Harry was a hard guy to stop. And once the others got going, too, I didn't know what to do, so I just went along with them. Actually, it was sort of funny."

Ardith seized her advantage. "Did you think it was funny when Harry caught you with a lolly trap? Was it funny when Harry started calling you 'Shit-Face Karlson'? Weren't you a little angry at him? I mean, *really* angry? Maybe furious?"

Chucky realized that Ardith knew about his grudge against Harry. Maybe she was fishing to see how deeply it ran. Could

Duster and Greg have told her about his argument with Harry before he headed down the lolly path? He cursed himself for not telling the whole truth back at Matulia. Now he felt trapped. No use trying to be evasive.

"No, it wasn't funny. It wasn't much fun getting called 'Shit-Face Karlson' every time I turned around."

Ardith stopped writing and looked out at the bay, taking nearly guilty pleasure in having trapped Karlson. It was time to move in, to close the deal. Her face became serene.

"Tell me what you know about the cover-up."

Chucky stalled. "The what?"

"The cover-up."

"What cover-up?"

"Look, when I interviewed you boys and the adult leaders at Matulia, you wouldn't tell me anything about Harry. Now I know you were hiding things. Why?"

Chucky looked down. More lies shattered. How much could he hold back?

"We couldn't talk to you about Harry. We promised the adult leaders we wouldn't say a word about our…you know, our stuff. We all pledged Scout's Honor."

"You pledged that you wouldn't tell me what?"

"The stuff about Harry. You know, depantsing Freddy Collins, setting the lolly trap, short sheeting, all that stuff."

"Not the blow job?"

"We didn't tell the adult leaders about that."

"Why not?"

"Because we promised Duster we wouldn't, under Scout's Honor. And we took a vow as Musketeers."

"You boys sure used Scout's Honor whenever it suited your purposes, didn't you?"

Ardith Cunningham slowly made notes, letting Chucky

squirm. Finally, she returned to her questioning. "Can you tell me anything more about the cover-up?"

The word "cover-up" again? What cover-up? Chucky struggled. Where the hell is she going with this?

"Look, I know there was a cover-up. You weren't the only one who told me about pledging Scout's Honor. So did Edward Marshall, your counselor. He actually broke down and cried when he told me. He admitted they had abused that pledge as part of the cover-up. Can you add to that?"

Chucky tried to shift the conversation back to her.

"Why do *you* think there was a cover-up? What do you think the adult leaders were trying to hide?"

"That's a good question," said Ardith. "Here are a couple of possibilities. Maybe you can help me sort them out. They might have been trying to protect the reputation of Troop 64. Or the image of the Boy Scouts."

"Look, Dr. Karlson, I'm not out to get the Scouts. They do wonderful work with boys. I can understand why they didn't want the community to learn about nut grabbing and lolly traps and blow jobs. I can understand why they didn't want to upset parents about camp safety. If those were the reasons, I can sympathize with them."

"And I don't think it was just the Troop 64 adult leaders," Ardith continued. "The Green River sheriff and coroner were involved. So were people at the *Kaioga City Tribune.* My editor refused to run the story the way I wrote it, with the bump on Harry's forehead. Can you add anything that might make things a little clearer?"

Karlson avoided the bump. "You're probably right about the scout leaders. They were really dedicated. They gave up two weeks of their vacations just to be with us, to help us. If there really was a cover-up, I'm sure they thought they were doing the right thing. Don't you?"

"You're probably right...unless..." Ardith focused on Chucky. "Unless they were covering up something else."

Chucky wasn't certain where this was going, but he had an unsettling premonition.

"Look, Dr. Karlson, I'm not going to make too much fun of you boys and Harry because you acted like a bunch of...well, you fill in the word. I told you I owed that to Ruth Vincent. But I also owe her something else. I owe her an effort—a real effort—to try to find out how Harry died." Ardith leaned forward, her face nearly touching his. "Chucky, what can you tell me about how Harry died?"

Chucky stared silently. He had no answer.

"Dr. Karlson, you're a physician, like the county coroner. Maybe Harry didn't just fall. Maybe someone hit him, like with a rock or a stick. That's how he got the bump on his forehead. Maybe some of the adults wanted to avoid bad publicity about Harry's death. It was bad enough that he died at camp. It would have been worse, much worse, if there were public suspicion that someone had killed him."

The word "killed" crawled up Chucky's spine. Killed was an awful word, the steppingstone to something even worse, like murdered.

"That would have been a good reason for the cover-up," Ardith continued. "It would help explain why the coroner mentioned but dismissed the bump on Harry's head, why the sheriff wouldn't investigate any further, and why my editor dropped the bump from my story."

"You can't be sure of that, can you?"

"No, but it makes sense. And it certainly fits with the facts."

"But you can't be sure!"

Ardith walked over to the window and admired the lights on the Golden Gate Bridge. The sun had long since disappeared. She decided it was time to pounce.

"OK, Dr. Karlson, I'm going to tell you exactly what I know.

I know that Harry Vincent pulled a lot of stuff. I know he made some people angry, very angry. In fact, as far as I can tell, he pissed off everyone in your tent, including you. I know that some of you said threatening things to him. I know that Harry died because he hit the back of his head when he fell. I know he also had a big bump on his forehead that he couldn't have gotten by falling on his back. You're a physician. Wouldn't you agree with what I've just laid out?"

"Yes, but that doesn't add up to anything certain."

"No, but it's factual. Now, what if the bump on his forehead came from somebody hitting him with a stick or a rock just before he fell? You can understand why the Scouts wouldn't want that kind of publicity about their camp, right?" Ardith paused.

"So let's take it one step further. What if the leaders had a suspicion about who might have hit Harry? What if someone had seen what happened to him and told the leaders and, for the good of the Scouts, they decided to hide it? Then it wouldn't just have been protecting the Scouts. It would have been covering up a killing, a crime."

Chucky was stunned by Ardith's ability to put these pieces together into a scenario that might have convinced a jury. But does she know something about the troop leaders' suspicions? Who told them? What? Or is she just bluffing?

Ardith picked up her pen and wrote slowly on her pad, fastidiously making large loops on her consonants. When she looked up, her face had turned to granite. "Benjamin Green told me you were the last person to see Harry Vincent alive." She waited for her words to sink in, then continued.

"Let me see if I've got this straight. The three of you were sitting in the Hawk tent after dinner. Harry got up to go to the lolly and you followed him. Is that correct?"

Chucky squirmed on the witness stand. "Yes, I wanted to talk to him."

"About what?"

"Look. I just wanted Harry to be more cooperative, to help me out with the patrol, to lay off Duster. He brushed me off."

"So that's when you started shouting at him. Benjamin Green heard you."

"I raised my voice, but I don't remember shouting at him."

"You don't remember?"

"I may have shouted, a little bit."

Chucky stalled, but he knew what was coming.

"What happened next?"

Chucky remembered very well. He knew what he saw, what he thought he saw, but he could only tell part of it.

"Harry headed down to the lolly."

"You didn't follow him?"

"Of course not!"

"Why of course not?"

"I didn't have to go to the lolly."

"So you just stood there at the top of the lolly path?"

"Well, I stood there trying to decide whether to go back to the tent or head for the campfire."

"Did anybody see you standing there?"

"Sure, Trent Georgis. He came up and we talked."

"Is there anybody else who can confirm that?"

Why in the hell did he need someone else to confirm it? What he said was true! Trent had interrupted him while he was watching Duster threaten Harry with a rock.

"No. Trent and I were alone. You can ask him."

"Trent Georgis died four years ago."

Trent Georgis dead? Oh, well, what difference does that make? Why in the hell should he, Charles Karlson, need an alibi. He hadn't done anything. The only thing he had done was try to protect his buddy, Duster Fertig.

"Look, Mrs. Cunningham, I've been telling you the truth, the whole truth. The last time I saw Harry alive was when we talked. Then he headed down to the lolly. The next time I saw him he was dead. Terry Fleener found him."

"Dr. Karlson," Ardith said slowly and precisely, "Terry Fleener was walking down to the outhouse when he found Harry. He didn't see anyone, just Harry's body. You seem to be the last person to have seen Vincent alive or..."

A rapturous sense of calm settled over Ardith Cunningham. It was worth all of the time she had spent setting the trap. She had nailed it. She had nailed him. Ardith looked at Karlson with an air of smugness as if she had gotten all she wanted, maybe more.

"Do you have anything more to add?"

"Look, you Windy City bitch, if you publish any of that stuff about me, I'm going to sue your butt until it's floating in Lake Michigan," Karlson wished he could say. But when he opened his mouth, all that came out was a soft "No," followed a few seconds later by "That's a lot of conjecture." That was as close as he could come to challenging her.

Their eyes met and froze. The words, "I've got one more thing to tell you. It's about Duster Fertig," rose to the top of his throat but wouldn't come out.

Ardith stowed her pen, finally, and placed her damn notepad in her briefcase. They didn't say another word, not even good-bye, as they walked down the hallway to the elevator.

Chucky retreated to his office. The murder suspect slumped into his chair. Fog had devoured the Golden Gate Bridge.

* * *

As the elevator door closed, Ardith felt a surge of joy, the joy of vindication and redemption. But eight floors later, when the elevator door opened, her joy had evaporated as she thought of Ruth Vincent reading a story about how her beloved son Harry may have been murdered at Matulia because the little cherub had made oodles of enemies with his disgusting antics.

For years, "little Ardie" had contemplated the pursuit of ultimate truth, the solving of the mystery, the settling of old scores, the quest for personal redemption, and the fulfillment of her unspoken moral pact with Ruth Vincent. Now, when it was time to write her story, the whole story, she recognized what a merciless dilemma she had inflicted upon herself.

# PART VI

# MOMENT OF TRUTH

# CHAPTER 50

• • • • • • • • •

# UNFINISHED STORIES

... *That is why I decided to revisit this story. That is why I had to retell this story, the whole story.*

*It's been thirty-six years since this spineless young reporter drove down to Hexterville, Missouri, a drive that would change her life and launch her career, a career spawned by her fear of standing up to her editor. It left me with still painful memories of having failed—failed myself, failed others—even as I became well known as a columnist and wrote three books, including my memoir, "Small Town Girl," in which I once again skirted the truth.*

*The story, my story, began in the summer of 1948 at Boy Scout Camp Matulia in ruggedly beautiful Southwest Missouri. Shrouded in the semi-darkness of nightfall, a young Boy Scout named Terry Fleener was walking down a hill toward a noxious six-seat outhouse when he stumbled over the dead body of another scout, Harry Vincent, and screamed "Oh, shit!" three times. That discovery set off a chain of events so bizarre that it has taken me nearly four decades to unravel everything that happened—at least almost everything. That search has relentlessly tested my investigative ability and perseverance. Here is that story, as well as the story of my seemingly endless quest to discover the truth.*

• • • • • • • • •

# CHAPTER 51

# REPRIEVE

By the time Charles Karlson, M.D., received his copy of *Unfinished Stories*, he had only one concern. Did Ardith Cunningham publicly accuse him of killing Harry Vincent? Or at least contributing to Harry's death?

While three patients waited unhappily in his reception room, Karlson raced through the chapter looking for the smoking gun. By the final page, the wise-cracking surgeon had succumbed to tears of relief. The smoking gun wasn't there. Chucky had escaped with only minor damage. Almost gleefully he informed Ginger Montadon that, yes, she would have scars from her upcoming neck surgery but, no, they would not be too visible.

After the last patient left, Charles returned to the chapter to make certain that he was in the clear. Correct! Cunningham had not accused him of murder. She had not even suggested any connection to Harry's death. She did mention that he was the last person known to have seen Harry alive, but she reported it in a flat, factual, non-accusatory manner. No need to think about suing her.

When Charles reread the chapter the next morning after surgery, his knowledge that he had avoided a direct accusation allowed him to focus on other matters. Liberated from the fear of suggested criminality, he now focused on his personal image. With that refocusing, anger replaced the previous day's "Wow, I've dodged a bullet" euphoria.

Fourteen-year-old Chucky Karlson emerged as a pretty un-savory young man. A weak patrol leader. A liar, although he wasn't alone in that. A poor role model who lacked respect for the use of Scout's Honor. Above all, a cloddish camp veteran who, like a naïve greenhorn, had stumbled into a lolly trap and had well earned his "Shit-Face Karlson" moniker.

For a few moments, Karlson felt like recanting his decision not to sue Cunningham, but he soon realized that this would probably just make matters worse. As things now stood, the *San Francisco Chronicle* might run a book review, maybe even with a specific mention of his portrayal. Given his local visi-bility, that wouldn't be surprising. But maybe not. Maybe they wouldn't even know the book had been published.

And if the *Chronicle* did review it, that was better than the newspaper carrying repeated stories about a prominent city orthopedic surgeon who was suing a highly respected journal-ist merely because she had exposed his youthful misdeeds. Of course, the columns would probably repeat her examples and he would come out looking like even more of a dork. So let it go. Who doesn't have a few youthful skeletons in his closet?

By the fourth reading, Charles could begin to look at the chapter through lenses other than his surprisingly fragile ego. That's when it struck him how different her written story was from the convoluted conspiracy theory, murder yarn, and per-sonal accusation that she had invented to crush him in his office.

Not that Cunningham allowed people, including Chucky, to come out unscathed. In fact, she described camp shenanigans with excruciating, explicit, and prurient detail. Depantsing. Nut grabbing. Short sheeting. Lolly traps. Blow jobs. She made them sound like a normal "boys will be boys" rite of passage, as natural as learning the alphabet or reciting the multiplica-tion tables.

Adults fared even worse. She skewered her newspaper editor, the Hexterville officials, and of course the scout leaders. Most of them emerged as incompetents, bullies, or feckless cowards, sometimes all three. Above all, they played free and loose with the truth, even using the Scout's Honor pledge to enforce lying. When caught up in a relentless, fast-moving situation beyond their capabilities, they simply lacked the right stuff.

The chapter portrayed these actions as individual character flaws, maybe the inevitable failures that came with being a human being. These were not institutional failures. In fact, Cunningham eulogized the Scouts for their contributions to the fostering of young men, and she made special mention of their thoughtfulness in awarding the Eagle Scout pin to the deceased Harry Vincent.

No convoluted conspiracy theory. The elaborate institutional cover-up that Cunningham had laid out for Chucky was nowhere to be found. Instead she portrayed the days following Harry Vincent's death as a parade not mainly of blatant lies but of half-truths, of incompetence in action, beginning with the coroner's report that mentioned the bump on Vincent's forehead but failed to explore the possible significance of its presence. Once the report had established accidental death as the operative truth, the scout leaders' efforts to control the camp's image seemed natural, maybe even laudable. Why rile up parents?

Charles shook his head, filled with new questions. Why had Cunningham's narrative changed so radically since her office diatribe? Why had she decided not to proclaim a conspiracy theory? Why had she downplayed the possibility of a killing?

The orthopedic surgeon methodically diagnosed the chapter. It took several readings for him to unravel the mystery, at least the mystery as he saw it. The key was Harry Vincent. Cunningham had virtually banished Harry from her new narrative.

Gone was the fun-loving Harry Vincent. Gone was the inventive kid who did crazy things. Gone was the charismatic prankster who regularly delighted people while sometimes infuriating them. In his place was flat, bland Scout Harry. Harry the dead body. Harry the posthumous recipient of an Eagle Scout pin. Harry the focus of a grieving mother.

A grin crossed Karlson's face. That strident bitch finally had to confront reality. He imagined Cunningham's growing frustration as interview after interview revealed that her imagined little cherub was actually a non-stop provocateur, that he caused trouble wherever he went, and that he made enemies almost without effort. This included enemies who might have contributed to his demise.

Ardith Cunningham, the relentless pursuer of pure truth, must have realized that she couldn't handle the truth. If she wrote the full truth that she had discovered in order to pursue her fantasies about murder and conspiracy, she would have to demolish the perfected public image of Eagle Scout Harry Vincent. And that would destroy the aging Kaioga City mother who had persevered through decades based on memory.

Ardith Cunningham had pursued the truth and, in the process, had trapped herself. She had uncovered a story she couldn't write. She had discovered a possible murder and maybe a conspiracy but, instead of revealing it, she had decided to join it. Fuck her.

* * *

Chucky called Duster.

"We dodged a bullet, didn't we, Porthos?"

"Did we ever."

"Do you think we've got anything more to worry about?"

"I would imagine not. After all, do you really think Ardith Cunningham wants to devote the rest of her life to a dead-end story that she can never really write?"

"I agree. Ruth Vincent is our ace in the hole."

Then came a chilling thought. Maybe Ruth Vincent's longevity was the only thing standing between them and Ardith's Cunningham's ferocity and determination to convict.

"You know, Duster, that other matter still bothers me."

"What other matter?"

"Who in the hell did I see arguing with Harry on the way down to the lolly?"

Duster paused before answering. "I don't imagine we'll ever know, Chucky. At this point, what difference does it make? It's over. Harry's gone."

But Chucky wasn't done. "Duster, do you really think Greg didn't see who hit Harry?"

Duster took a deep breath. "I've been thinking about that, too. If Greg wanted to tell us, he probably would have."

Duster's "probably" sounded ominous, so Chucky let it drop. But he also realized that he would probably spend the rest of his life reconstructing that day at Camp Matulia. Harry was gone, but Chucky knew that he would never stop pondering the mystery: Who had killed him?

• • • • • • • • •

# CHAPTER 52

# ADULATION

Ardith Cunningham sifted through the stacks piled high on her desk. Ecstatic reviews. Enthusiastic letters from colleagues and admirers. Kind notes from friends. Prizes would likely ensue.

Yet her eyes kept returning to one unopened letter. She picked it up, stared at the tiny handwritten return address, *R. Vincent,* and then laid it back down as she had been doing almost daily for more than a week. Finally she picked it up and slid it into the bottom desk drawer with the other unopened letters from Kaioga City.

• • • • • • • • •

# CHAPTER 53

# CONTEMPLATION

Day after day, Chucky Karlson found himself reliving Camp Matulia, pondering the list of possible suspects. Duster. Greg. Flipper. Freddy. Putz Perryman. That guy sure had good reason to be furious at Harry. Whatever, Harry was gone. Duster, Greg, and he had patched things up, sort of, but it would never be the same as back in the good old days. Not much left of the Musketeers.

Again and again, Chucky tried to visualize that early evening at the camp. There was Harry Vincent's anguished face. There was that raised arm holding a rock. And there was the broad back and the big neck. Sometimes he would focus tightly on that single image and try, with everything he had, to determine definitively who it might have been. But no matter how wide a net he cast, his mind always returned to the same place: Duster's thick neck.

Many times he would pick up the phone to call Greg Brooks, to question him about what he'd seen, what he'd really seen. Now and then he actually punched in a few numbers. But he always ended by putting the phone back on the hook, sometimes slamming it.

Maybe he should just try to put Matulia behind him, for good, and focus on the future. Forget Merona and Kaioga City. He had survived them. How good it was being Charles Karlson, M.D., of San Francisco.

. . . . . . . . .

# CHAPTER 54

# REQUIEM

Ardith Cunningham knew this day would arrive. It had. She reread the obituary. Ruth Vincent, mother of Harry Vincent, who had received a posthumous Eagle Scout award following his 1948 death at Camp Matulia, had died peacefully in her sleep in Kaioga City. She is survived by one living family member, a younger sister, Marjorie Higgins. In lieu of flowers, donations can be made to Presbyterian Hospital of Kaioga City.

Ardith glanced at the first of several gray, five-drawer metal files. Her eyes focused on the second drawer from the bottom, a drawer labeled Harry Vincent, a drawer crammed with notes, drafts, documents, and interviews. She took out a light blue envelope and extracted a dog-eared manuscript. The title page read *Who Murdered Harry Vincent?*

When Ardith began reading, the sun was beating down on the Chicago streets. By the time she had finished, the moon had risen over Lake Michigan. Then, with a relieved smile, she began making notes.

# ABOUT THE AUTHOR

• • • • • • • • • • • • •

**Carlos E. Cortés** is the Edward A. Dickson Emeritus Professor of History at the University of California, Riverside. His books include his memoir, *Rose Hill: An Intermarriage before Its Time* and an award-winning book of poetry, *Fourth Quarter: Reflections of a Cranky Old Man*. Cortés served as Cultural Consultant for the Dreamworks film, *Puss in Boots: The Last Wish* and received the 2009 NAACP Image Award for being the Creative/Cultural Advisor for Nickelodeon's *Dora the Explorer* and *Go, Diego, Go!*. He also travels the country performing his one-person autobiographical play, "A Conversation with Alana: One Boy's Multicultural Rite of Passage."

# SELECTED INLANDIA BOOKS

• • • • • • • • • • • • • • • • • • •

*Search Party* by René Solívan

*Razed* by Thatcher Carter

*Keep Sweet* by Victoria Waddle

*Lost in the Wilderness: Ansel Adams and the 1960s* by Douglas McCulloh

*Apartness: A Memoir in Essays and Poems* by Judy Kronenfeld

*Desert Forest: Life with Joshua Trees* by Sant Khalsa and Juniper Harrower

*Guajira, the Cuba girl* by Zita Arocha

*Breaking Pattern* by Tisha Marie Reichle-Aguilera

*Exit Prohibited* by Ellen Estilai

*These Black Bodies Are...*, edited by Romaine Washington

*The Vermillion Speedateer* by Sebraé Harris

*Pretend Plumber* by Stephanie Barbé Hammer

*Ladybug* by Nikia Chaney

*Vital: The Future of Healthcare*, edited by RM Ambrose

*Portrait Of A Community: Selections From The Chaffey Community Museum Of Art* by Wendy Slatkin

*Güero-Güero: The White Mexican and Other Published and Unpublished Stories* by Dr. Eliud Martínez

*A Short Guide to Finding Your First Home in the United States: An Inlandia anthology on the immigrant experience*, Inlandia editorial board

*Care: Stories* by Christopher Records

*San Bernardino, Singing*, edited by Nikia Chaney

*Facing Fire: Art, Wildfire, and the End of Nature in the New West* by Douglas McCulloh

*Writing from Inlandia*, an annual anthology (2011–)

*In the Sunshine of Neglect: Defining Photographs and Radical Experiments in Inland Southern California,1950 to the Present* by Douglas McCulloh

*Henry L. A. Jekel: Architect of Eastern Skyscrapers and the California Style* by Dr. Vincent Moses and Catherine Whitmore

*Orangelandia: The Literature of Inland Citrus* edited by Gayle Brandeis

*While We're Here We Should Sing* by The Why Nots

*Go to the Living* by Micah Chatterton

*No Easy Way: Integrating Riverside Schools - A Victory for Community* by Arthur L. Littleworth

# ABOUT INLANDIA INSTITUTE

• • • • • • • • • • • • • • • • • • • •

The Inlandia Institute is a regional literary non-profit and publishing house. We seek to bring focus to the richness of the literary enterprise that has existed in this region for ages.

The mission of Inlandia Books is to recognize, support, and expand literary activity in Inland Southern California by publishing works which deepen people's awareness, understanding, and appreciation of this unique, complex and creatively vibrant region. The mission is carried out by actively seeking out new works by writers who are affiliated with the region, and also through national literary competitions which elevate Inlandia Books to the national literary stage.

To learn more about the Inlandia Institute, please visit our website at www.InlandiaInstitute.org.

www.ingramcontent.com/pod-product-compliance
Lightning Source LLC
Chambersburg PA
CBHW041751010726
47507CB00009B/360